Pilgrims

Pilgrims

ELIZABETH
GILBERT

HOUGHTON MIFFLIN COMPANY

BOSTON ✦ NEW YORK

1997

For information about permission to reproduce
selections from this book, write to
Permissions, Houghton Mifflin Company,
215 Park Avenue South, New York,
New York 10003.

Library of Congress Cataloging-in-Publication Data
Gilbert, Elizabeth, date.
Pilgrims / Elizabeth Gilbert.
p.   cm.
ISBN 0-395-83623-9
1. United States — Social life and customs —
20th century — Fiction.
I. Title.
PS3557.I3415P55 1997
813'.54 — dc21   97-19956 CIP

Printed in the United States of America

Book design by Robert Overholtzer

QUM 10 9 8 7 6 5 4 3 2 1

"Pilgrims" first appeared in *Esquire*. "Elk Talk" first
appeared in *Story*. "Tall Folks" first appeared in *Mississippi
Review*. "The Names of Flowers and Girls" first
appeared in *Ploughshares*. "The Famous Torn and Restored
Lit Cigarette Trick" first appeared in *Paris Review*.
"The Finest Wife" first appeared in *Story*.

FOR MOM AND DAD
WITH MUCH LOVE

Whan that April with his showres soote
The drought of March hath perced to the roote
And bathed every vein in swich licour,
Of which vertu engendred is the flowr;
Whan Zephyrus, eek, with his sweete breeth
Inspired hath in every holt and heeth
The tender croppes, and the yonge sunne
Hath in the Ram his halve course y-runne,
And smalle fowles maken melodye
That sleepen all the night with open ye
(So pricketh hem Nature in hir corages),
Than longen folk to goon on pilgrimages . . .

— GEOFFREY CHAUCER

CONTENTS

Contents

Pilgrims

Pilgrims

✦ ✦ ✦

WHEN MY OLD MAN said he'd hired her, I said, "A girl?"
A girl, when it wasn't that long ago women couldn't
work on this ranch even as cooks, because the wran-
glers got shot over them too much. They got shot even over the
ugly cooks. Even over the old ones.

I said, "A girl?"

"She's from Pennsylvania," my old man said. "She'll be good
at this."

"She's from what?"

When my brother Crosby found out, he said, "Time for me
to find new work when a girl starts doing mine."

My old man looked at him. "I heard you haven't come over
Dutch Oven Pass once this season you haven't been asleep on
your horse or reading a goddamn book. Maybe it's time for you
to find new work anyhow."

He told us that she showed up somehow from Pennsylvania
in the sorriest piece of shit car he'd ever seen in his life. She
asked him for five minutes to ask for a job, but it didn't take that
long. She flexed her arm for him to feel, but he didn't feel it. He
liked her, he said, right away. He trusted his eye for that, he said,
after all these years.

"You'll like her, too," he said. "She's sexy like a horse is sexy. Nice and big. Strong."

"Eighty-five of your own horses to feed, and you still think horse is sexy," I said, and my brother Crosby said, "I think we got enough of that kind of sexy around here already."

She was Martha Knox, nineteen years old and tall as me, thick-legged but not fat, with cowboy boots that anyone could see were new that week, the cheapest in the store and the first pair she'd ever owned. She had a big chin that worked only because her forehead and nose worked, too, and she had the kind of teeth that take over a face even when the mouth is closed. She had, most of all, a dark brown braid that hung down the center of her back, thick as a girl's arm.

I danced with Martha Knox one night early in the season. It was a day off to go down the mountain, get drunk, make phone calls, do laundry, fight. Martha Knox was no dancer. She didn't want to dance with me. She let me know this by saying a few times that she wasn't going to dance with me, and then, when she finally agreed, she wouldn't let go of her cigarette. She held it in one hand and let that hand fall and not be available. So I kept my beer bottle in one hand, to balance her out, and we held each other with one arm each. She was no dancer and she didn't want to dance with me, but we found a good slow sway anyway, each of us with an arm hanging down, like a rodeo cowboy's right arm, like the right arm of a bull rider, not reaching for anything. She wouldn't look anywhere but over my left shoulder, like that part of her that was a good dancer with me was some part she had not ever met and didn't feel like being introduced to.

My old man also said this about Martha Knox: "She's not beautiful, but I think she knows how to sell it."

Well, it's true that I wanted to hold her braid. I always had wanted to from first seeing it and mostly I wanted to in that dance, but I didn't reach for it and I didn't set down my beer bottle. Martha Knox wasn't selling anything.

We didn't dance again that night or again at all, because it was a long season and my old man worked all of us too hard. There were no more full days off for dancing or fighting. And when we would sometimes get an afternoon off in the middle of a hard week, we would all go to the bunkhouse and sleep; fast, dead tired sleep, in our own bunks, in our own boots, like firemen or soldiers.

Martha Knox asked me about rodeo. "Crosby says it's a good way to get made dead," she said.

"It's the best way I know."

We were facing each other across the short pine fire, just us, drinking. In the tent behind Martha Knox were five hunters from Chicago, asleep or tired, mad at me for not being able to make them good enough shots to kill any of the elk we'd seen that week. In the tent behind me were the cook stoves and the food and two foam pads with a sleeping bag for each of us. She slept under horse blankets to be warmer, and we both slept on the jeans we'd be wearing the next day, to keep them from freezing. It was the middle of October, the last hunt of the season, and ice hung in long needles off the muzzles of the horses every morning when we saddled.

"Are you drunk?" I asked her.

"I'll tell you something," she said. "That's a pretty damn good question."

She was looking at her hands. They were clean, with all the expected cuts and burns, but they were clean hands.

"You rode rodeo, right?" she asked.

"One time too many," I said.

"Bulls?"

"Broncs."

"Is that why you get called Buck?"

"I get called Buck because I stabbed myself in the leg with my buck knife when I was a kid."

"Ever get nailed in rodeo?"

"I got on this bronc one night and knew right away, right in the chute, that it wasn't going to have me. It wanted me gone and dead for trying. Never was so scared on a horse as on that son of a bitch."

"You think it knew?"

"Knew? How could it know?"

"Crosby says the first job of a horse is to figure out who's riding it and who's in charge."

"That's my old man's line. He says it to scare dudes. If horses were that smart, they'd be riding us."

"That's Crosby's line."

"No." I took another drink. "That's my old man's line, too."

"So you got thrown."

"But my wrist got caught in the rigging and I got dragged around the ring three times under the son of a bitch's belly. Crowd loved it. Horse loved it. Put me in the hospital almost a year."

"Give me that?" She reached for the bottle. "I want to ride broncs," she said. "I want to ride rodeo."

"That's what I meant to do," I said. "I meant to talk you into it with that story."

"Was your dad mad?"

I didn't answer that. I stood up and walked over to the tree where all the pack gear was hung up in the branches, like food hung away from bears. I unzipped my fly and said, "Shield your eyes, Martha Knox, I'm about to unleash the biggest thing in the Wyoming Rockies."

She didn't say anything while I pissed, but when I got back to the fire she said, "That's Crosby's line."

I found a can of tobacco in my pocket. "No, it's not," I said. "That's my old man's line, too."

I tapped the can against my leg to pack the chew, then took some. It was my last can of tobacco, almost empty.

"My old man bought that bronc," I said. "He found the owner and gave him twice what the bastard was worth. Then he took it out back of the cook shack, shot it in the head, and buried it in the compost pile."

"You're kidding me," Martha Knox said.

"Don't bring it up with him."

"Hell no. No way."

"He came to see me every day in the hospital. We never even talked because he was so goddamn beat. He just smoked. He'd flick the cigarette butts over my head and they'd land in the toilet and hiss out. I was in a neck brace for a bunch of months and I couldn't even turn my head and see him. So damn bored. Just about the only thing I lived for was seeing those butts go flying over my face to the toilet."

"That's bored," Martha Knox said.

"My brother Crosby showed up sometimes, too, with pictures of girls."

"Sure."

"Well, that was okay to look at, too."

"Sure. Everyone had a butt for you to look at."

She drank. I took the bottle, passed it back, and she drank more. There was snow around us. There'd been hail on the day we rode in and snow almost every night. In the afternoons big patches of it would melt off in the meadow and leave small white piles like laundry, and the horses would walk through these. The grass was almost gone, and the horses had started leaving at night, looking for better food. We hung cowbells around their necks, and these rang flat and loud while they grazed. It was a good noise. I was used to it, and I only noticed it when it was gone. That quiet of no bells meant no horses, and it could wake me up in the middle of the night. We'd have to go out after the horses then, but I knew where they usually went, and we'd head that way. Martha Knox was figuring them out, too, and she didn't complain about having to get dressed in the middle of the night in the cold and go listen for bells in the dark. She liked it. She was getting it.

"You know something about your brother Crosby?" Martha Knox asked. "He really thinks he knows his way around a girl."

I didn't say anything, and she went on. "Now how can that be, Buck, when there aren't any girls around?"

"Crosby knows girls," I said. "He lived in towns."

"What towns? Casper? Cheyenne?"

"Denver. Crosby lived in Denver."

"Okay, Denver."

"Well, there's a girl or two in Denver."

"Sure." She yawned.

"So he could have learned his way around girls in Denver."

"I see that, Buck."

"Girls love Crosby."

"I bet."

"They do. Me and Crosby are going down to Florida one of these winters and wreck every marriage we can. There's a lot of rich women down there. A lot of rich, bored women."

"They'd have to be pretty bored," Martha Knox said, and laughed. "They'd have to be bored to goddamn tears."

"You don't like my brother Crosby?"

"I love your brother Crosby. Why wouldn't I like Crosby? I think Crosby's the greatest."

"Good for you."

"But he thinks he knows his way around a girl, and that's a pain in the ass."

"Girls love Crosby."

"I showed him a picture of my sister one time. He told me she looked like she'd been on the wrong side of a lot of bad dick. What kind of a thing to say is that?"

"You have a sister?"

"Agnes. She works in Missoula."

"On a ranch?"

"Not on a ranch, no. She's a stripper, actually. She hates it because it's a college town. She says college boys don't tip, no matter what you stick in their faces."

"Did you ever fool around with my brother Crosby?" I asked.

"Hey, Buck," she said. "Don't be shy. Ask whatever's on your mind."

"Oh, shit. Never mind."

"You know what they called me in high school? Fort Knox. You know why? Because I wouldn't let anyone in my pants."

"Why not?"

"Why not?" Martha Knox poked at the fire with a twig, then threw the twig in. She moved the coffee pot away from the flames and tapped the side of it with a spoon to settle the grounds that were boiling. "Why not? Because I didn't think it was a very good idea."

"That's a hell of a nickname."

"Buck's a better one."

"Taken," I said.

Martha Knox got up and went into the tent, and when she came out she had an armful of wood. I asked, "What are you doing?"

"The fire is almost dead."

"So let it die. It's late."

She didn't answer me.

"I have to get up at three-thirty tomorrow morning," I said.

"So good night."

"And so do you have to get up."

Martha Knox put a stick on the fire and sat down. "Buck," she said, "don't be a baby." She took a long drink and she sang, "Mama, don't let your cowboys grow up to be babies . . ."

"That's a Crosby line," I said.

"Let me ask you something, Buck. When we're done up here, let me go hunting with you and Crosby."

"I don't think my old man would be crazy about that."

"I didn't ask to go hunting with your old man."

"He won't like it."

"Why?"

"You ever even shoot a gun?"

"Sure. When I was a little kid my parents sent me out to Montana to stay with my dad's uncle for the summer. I called my folks after a few weeks and said, 'Uncle Earl set up a coffee can on a log and let me shoot at it and I hit the goddamn thing six times.' They made me come home early. Didn't like the sound of that."

"Doesn't sound like your old man's going to be too crazy about it either, then."

"We do not not have to worry about my father," she said. "Not anymore."

"That so?"

She took her hat off and set it on her leg. It was an old hat. It belonged once to my cousin Rich. My old man gave it to Martha Knox. He steamed a new shape into it over a coffee pot one morning, put a neat crease in the top. The hat fit her. It suited her.

"Now listen, Buck," she said. "This is a good story, and you'll like it. My dad grew Christmas trees. Not a lot of them. He grew exactly fifty Christmas trees and he grew them for ten years. In our front yard. Trimmed them all the time with kitchen scissors, so they were pretty, but only about this tall."

Martha Knox held her hand about three feet off the ground.

"Problem is we lived in the country," she went on. "Everybody had woods in their back yards. Nobody ever bought a Christmas tree in that place. So this wasn't a good business idea, fifty perfect trees. No big money there. But that's what he did, and my mom worked." She took her hat off her leg and put it back on. "Anyway. He opened up for business last December and nobody showed up and he thought that was pretty damn weird, because they were such nice trees. He went out drinking. Me and my sister, we cut down maybe twenty of the fuckers. Threw them in the station wagon. Drove an hour to the highway, started flagging down cars and giving trees away. Anyone who stops gets a free tree. It was like . . . Well, hell. It was like Christmas."

Martha Knox found a cigarette in her coat pocket and lit it.

"Now," she said. "We drive home. There's my dad. He pushes Agnes down and hauls off and punches me in the face."

"He ever hit you before?" I asked, and she shook her head.

"And he never will again, either."

She looked at me, cool and even. I looked at her smoking her cigarette two thousand miles from home, and I thought about her shooting the goddamn coffee can six times, and we were quiet for a long time before I said, "You didn't kill him, did you?"

She didn't look away and she didn't answer fast, but she said, "Yeah. I killed him."

"Jesus Christ," I said finally. "Jesus son-of-a-bitching Christ."

Martha Knox handed the bottle to me, but I didn't take it. She came over beside me and sat down. She put her hand on my leg.

"Jesus Christ," I said again. "Jesus son-of-a-bitching Christ."

She sighed. "Buck," she said. "Honey." She patted my leg and then she nudged me. "You are the most gullible man I know on this planet."

"Fuck you."

"I shot my dad and buried him in the compost pile. Don't tell anyone, okay?"

"Fuck you, Martha Knox."

She got up and sat down on the other side of the fire again. "It was a great night, though. Lying in the driveway on my back with a bloody nose. I knew I was out of there."

She handed me the bottle again, and this time I drank. We did not talk for a long time, but we finished off the bottle, and when the fire got low, Martha Knox put more wood on it. I had my feet so close to the flames that the soles of my boots started to smoke, so I moved back, but not much. In October up there it isn't easy to be warm and I would not pull away from that kind of heat too fast.

There were bells from the meadow of horses moving but not leaving, grazing bells ringing, good bells. I could have named every horse out there and guessed who every horse was standing next to because of the way they liked to pair, and I could have told how each horse rode and how its mother and father rode, too. There were elk out there, still, but they were moving lower, like the horses wanted to move, for better food. Bighorn sheep and bear and moose were out there, too, all of them moving down, and I was listening for all of them. This night was clear. No clouds, except the fast clouds of our own breath, gone by the next breath, and it was bright from an almost finished moon.

"Listen," I said, "I was thinking of going for a ride."

"Now?" Martha Knox asked, and I nodded, but she had already known that I meant now, yes, now. Before she'd even asked, she was already looking at me and weighing things, mostly the big rule of my old man, which was this: no joy-riding during work, not ever. No play-riding, no night-riding, no dare-riding, no dumb-riding, no risk-riding, not ever, not, most of all, during hunting camp. Before she'd even asked,

"Now?" she'd thought of that, and she'd thought also that we were tired and drunk. There were hunters asleep in the tent behind her, and she thought of that, too. And I had also thought of all that.

"Okay," she said.

"Listen," I said, and I leaned in closer to the fire which was between us. "I was thinking of going up Washakee Pass tonight."

I watched her. I knew she'd never been out that far, but she knew what it was, because Washakee was the only way for miles in any direction to get over the Continental Divide and into the middle of the Rockies. My brother Crosby called it the Spine. It was narrow and iced, and it pushed thirteen thousand feet, but it went over and in, and Martha Knox had not ever gone that far.

"Okay," she said. "Let's go."

"Well, listen. I was thinking of not stopping there."

She didn't stop looking at me, and she didn't change her expression, which was the expression of a good hunter watching for a good shot coming. Then I told her.

"We take a pack horse each and whatever food and gear fits on them. I ride Stetson, you ride Jake, and we don't come back."

"I'll ride Handy."

"Not that spotted-ass cocksucker."

"I'll ride Handy," she said again, and I had forgotten that she had talked my old man into selling her that crazy horse.

"Okay. But he's all wrong for this."

"What about the hunters?"

"They'll be fine, if they don't freak out."

"They'll freak out."

"They'll be fine."

"Talk about a bunch of pilgrims, Buck," she said. "These guys have never even been in a back yard."

"If they're smart, they'll hike out tomorrow as soon as they figure we're gone. The trail's marked like a goddamn freeway. They'll be fine. The soonest they'll get to the ranch is tomorrow night, late. The soonest the forest service could come after us is the next day. If we ride straight, we could be ninety miles south by then."

"Tell me you're dead serious," Martha Knox said. "Because I'll do this."

"I figure four or five days until we get to the Uinta range, and if they don't catch us before then, they'll never catch us."

"Okay. Let's do this."

"Then we head south. And we'll have to, because of winter. There's no reason in the world we shouldn't be in Mexico in a few months."

"Let's do it."

"Jesus Christ. I've got it all figured out. Jesus son-of-a-bitching Christ. We'll steal cattle and sheep and sell them at all those puny mountain outfits where nobody ever asks any questions."

"Buck," she said.

"And we'll ride into all those puny foothill towns in Utah and Wyoming and we'll hold up their banks. On horseback."

"Buck," she said again.

"It must be a hundred years since anyone held up a bank on goddamn horseback. They won't know how to deal with us. They'll be chasing us in cars, and there we go, over the guard-rails, back up the mountains with all that cash. Gone."

"Buck," she said, and I still didn't answer, but this time I stopped talking.

"Buck," she said. "You're just full of shit, aren't you?"

"I figure we can last four or five months before we finally get gunned down."

"You're just full of shit. You're not going anywhere."

"You think I wouldn't do something like that?"

"I don't even want to talk about it."

"You think I wouldn't do that?"

"You want to take off with some horses and see if we get made dead out there? Fine, I'm all for that. But don't waste my time with this outlaw bullshit."

"Come on," I said. "Come on, Martha Knox."

"You're just limited. Limited."

"You wouldn't just take off like that anyway."

She looked at me like she was going to say something mean and mad, but instead she got up and poured the coffee over what was left of the fire to put it out.

"Come on, Martha Knox," I said.

She sat down again, but I couldn't see her well in the new dark, over the wet ash.

"Don't waste my time like that again," she said.

"Come on. You can't just take off like that."

"The hell I can't."

"You would've just stolen my old man's horses?"

"Handy is my goddamn horse."

"Come on, Martha Knox," I said, but she stood up and went into the tent behind me. Then the tent was lit from inside, the way it was on mornings before the sun was up, when she would make day packs for the hunt, and from the meadow where I was starting to saddle I would see the tent glowing, but barely, because it was just one lantern she used.

I waited, and she came out of the tent with that lantern. She also had a bridle, taken from the hook by the cook stoves where we hung all the bridles, so that the bits would not be frozen with dew, so the bits would not be ice in the horses' mouths in the mornings. She walked past me toward the meadow. She walked fast like always, and, like always, she walked like a boy.

I went after her. I stumbled on a loose rock, and I caught her arm. "You're not taking off by yourself," I said.

"Yes, I am. I'm going to Mexico. In the middle of the night. Just me and this bridle."

Then she said, "I'm kidding, Buck," even though I hadn't answered her.

I held her arm and we walked. The ground was rough, wet in some parts and in other parts covered with thin snow. We tripped ourselves up on rocks and fell into each other but didn't fall over, and the lantern helped some. We followed bells until we were with the horses. Martha Knox set the lantern on a stump. We looked at the horses and they looked at us. Some of them moved away, moved sideways or back from us. But Stetson came over to me. I put my hand out and he sniffed at it and set his chin on it. He moved off and bent to graze again, and the bell around his neck rang like that move had been important, but the bells rang always, and it was nothing.

Martha Knox was in the horses, saying the things we always say to horses, saying, "Hey, there, steady now, easy buddy," like the words get understood, when really it's only the voice that matters, and the words could be any words.

She found Handy and I watched her bridle him. I watched him let her bridle him, and the spots over his back and rump in the almost dark were ugly, like accidental spots, like mistakes. I went over and she was talking to Handy and buckling the bridle by his ear.

I said, "You know my old man got this horse from its owner for a hundred dollars, the guy hated it so bad."

"Handy's the best. Look at those pretty legs."

"My old man says they should've named him Handful."

"Should've named him Handsome," she said, and I laughed, but I laughed too loud, and Handy jerked his head back.

"Easy there," she told him. "Steady now; easy boy."

"You know why Indians rode appaloosas into battle?" I asked.

"Yes. I do."

"So they'd be good and pissed off when they got there."

Martha Knox said, "You want to take a guess how many times I've heard that joke this summer?"

"I hate an appaloosa. I hate them all."

She stood next to Handy and ran her palm down his spine. She took the reins and a bunch of mane and pushed herself up on him, fast, just like I'd taught her in June. He danced back a few steps, but she reined him, she touched his neck, she stopped him.

"You coming or not?" she asked.

"You couldn't pay me enough to ride that spotted-ass cock-sucker."

"Get up here."

"He won't take two bareback."

"He'll take two. Get up here."

"Steady boy," I said, and got myself up on him, behind Martha Knox. He danced sideways before I was settled, but this time she let him dance and then she kicked him and he was in a loose trot already while I was reaching around her waist with both arms, reaching for handfuls of mane. She let him trot and then he slowed and walked. She let him walk where he wanted to, and he circled the lantern twice and lazy. He sniffed at a mare, who moved fast from him. He walked to a tree and stood under it, still.

"Hell of a ride," I said.

She kicked him, not a nudging kick this time, but a serious one, and he took off from the kick and in two more kicks was running wide open. We were too drunk for it, and it was too dark for it, and there were too many things in that meadow for a horse to trip over, but we were running wide open. His bell and hooves were loud, and they were a surprise to the other horses, who scattered behind us. I heard a few of them follow us, belled and fast.

Martha Knox had reins, but she wasn't using them, and my hat was gone, and so was hers, blown off. Handy might have stumbled or he might have kicked funny the way horses who love to run sometimes kick, or we might have been settled wrong, but we fell. With my arms still around her, we went over together, so who could say who fell first, or whose fault? That meadow was the best place for horses on long trips, but by this hunt it was spent. The next spring it would be different, with new grass wet from runoff, but that night it was packed dirt and frozen, and we hit it hard. We took the same fall, both of us. We took the fall in our hips and our shoulders. I knew I wasn't hurt and guessed she wasn't, but before I could ask, she was laughing.

"Oh, man," she said. "Goddamn."

I pulled my arm out from under her and rolled off my hip onto my back, and she rolled onto her back, too. We were far from any lantern, but the moon was big and lit. I turned my head to see Martha Knox's face by my face. Her hat was gone, and she was rubbing her arm, but she wasn't looking anywhere but right up at the sky, the kind of sky we don't see too much of, because of trees or bad weather, or because we sleep or stare at fires instead.

Handy came back — first his bell, then his huge face over our faces, hot and close. He smelled at us like we were plants or maybe something he would want.

"You're a good horse, Handy," Martha Knox said, not with the voice we always use for horses, but with her normal voice, and she meant it. I didn't think she wanted me to kiss her, although it was true that I wanted to kiss her then. She looked great. On that frozen dead ground, she looked as good and important as new grass or berries.

"You're a good horse," she told Handy again, and she sounded very sure of that. He smelled her again, carefully.

I looked up, too, at the sky, and the stars were no stars I hadn't seen before, but they seemed closer and unfamiliar. I watched long enough to see one of them drop above us, long and low. That's common to see in a good sky out here. This one star, though, left a slow thin arc, like a cigarette still burning flung over our heads. If Martha Knox saw this, it was only as she was reaching up already with one hand for her horse's reins, and it wasn't something she mentioned.

Elk Talk

◆   ◆   ◆

BENNY had been living with Ed and Jean for over a year. His mother was Jean's sister, and she was still in a hospital bed in Cheyenne, comatose, because she had driven her car into a snowplow on her way home from an art class one night. Jean had offered to take in her eight-year-old nephew as soon as she'd been told about the accident, and the whole family had agreed that such an arrangement would be best for Benny. When people asked Jean where Benny's father was, she said simply, "He's not available at this time," as if he were a business-man unable to come to the telephone.

Ed and Jean had a daughter of their own, married and living in Ohio, and when they moved from town into the mountain cabin, they were not expecting to share it someday with a child. Yet Benny was there now, and every morning Jean drove five miles down the dirt road so that he could meet his school bus. Every afternoon she met him at the same place. It was more difficult in the winter, on account of the heavy, inevitable snow, but they'd managed.

Ed worked for the Fish and Game Department, and had a large green truck with the state emblem on its doors. He was semiretired, and in recent months had developed something of a belly, round and firm as a pregnant teenager's. When he was home, he cut and stacked firewood or worked on the cabin. They were always insulating it more, always discovering and fixing flaws to make themselves more resistant to winter. Jean canned and froze vegetables from her garden in July and August, and when she went for walks she picked up small dry sticks along the path to bring home and save for kindling. The cabin was only a small place, with a short back porch facing the woods. Jean had converted the living room into a bedroom for Benny, and he slept on the couch under a down quilt.

It was the end of October, and Ed was gone for the weekend, giving a speech about poaching at some convention in Jackson. Jean was driving to pick up Benny at the bus stop when a station wagon approached her, speeding, pulling behind it a large camper. She swerved quickly, barely avoiding an accident, wincing as the side of her car scraped the underbrush to her right. Safely past, she glanced in the rearview mirror and tried to make out the receding tail end of the camper through the thick dust just lifted.

She couldn't remember the last time she'd met a car on that road. Ed and Jean had the only house for miles, and traffic consisted of the occasional truckload of hunters, or perhaps a teenage couple looking for a secluded parking spot. There was no reason for a station wagon with a camper to come out here. She imagined that it was a vacationing family, lost on their way to Yellowstone, miserable children in the back and a father driving, refusing to stop for directions. At such a speed, he would kill them all.

Benny's bus was early that day, and when Jean reached the highway, he was waiting for her, holding his lunch box close to his chest, standing scarcely taller than the mailbox beside him.

"I changed my mind," he said when he got into the car. "I want to be a karate man."

"But we already have your costume ready, Benny."

"It's not a real costume. It's just my Little League uniform, that's all."

"Ben. You wanted to wear it. That's what you told me you wanted to be for Halloween."

"I want to be a karate man," he repeated. He didn't whine, but spoke slowly and loudly, the way he always did, as if everyone in his life was hard of hearing or a beginning student of the English language.

"Well, I'm sorry. You can't be one," Jean said. "It's too late to make a new costume now."

Benny looked out the window and crossed his arms. After a few minutes, he said, "I sure wish I could be a karate man."

"Help me out, Ben? Don't make things so hard, okay?"

He didn't answer, but sighed resignedly, like somebody's mother. Jean drove in silence, more slowly than usual, keeping the speeding station wagon in mind at each curve. About halfway home, she asked, "Did you have art class today, Benny?"

He shook his head.

"No? Did you have gym class, then?"

"No," Benny said. "We had music."

"Music? Did you learn any new songs?"

He shrugged.

"Why don't you sing me what you learned today?"

Benny said nothing, and Jean repeated, "Why don't you sing me what you learned today? I'd like to hear your new songs."

After another silence, Benny pulled a blue-gray wad of chewing gum from his mouth and stuck it on the handle of his lunch box. Then, gazing solidly at the windshield, he recited in a low monotone, "There was a farmer had a dog and Bingo was his name oh. B-I-N-G-O," he spelled, carefully enunciating each letter. "B-I-N-G-O. B-I-N-G-O. And Bingo," Benny said, "was his name. Oh."

He peeled the gum off his lunch box and returned it to its place in his mouth.

That night after dinner, Jean helped Benny into his Little League uniform and cut strips of reflecting tape to lay over the numbers on the back of his jersey.

"Do you have to do that?" he asked.

"I want cars to see you as well as you see them," she said.

He accepted this without further protest. Having won an earlier dispute about the wearing of a hat and gloves, he let her have this one. Jean found the old Polaroid camera in her desk drawer and brought it into the living room.

"We'll take a picture to show Uncle Ed when he gets home," she said. "You look so nice. He'll want to see."

She found him in the tiny square of the viewfinder, and backed up until he was completely framed.

"Smile," she said. "Here we go."

He did not blink, not even during the flash, but stood in place and smiled at the last moment, as a favor to her. They both watched as the camera slowly pushed out the cloudy, damp photograph.

"Hold this by the edges carefully," Jean instructed, handing it to Benny, "and see what turns up."

There was a knock at the door. Jean stood up quickly, startled. She glanced at Benny, who was holding the developing picture between his thumb and forefinger, looking at her in anxious surprise.

"Stay there," she told him, and walked to the window at the back of the cabin. It was dark already, and she had to press her face close against the cold glass to see the vague figures on the porch. There was another knock, and a high voice, muffled through the thick oak, called, "Trick or treat!"

Jean opened the door and saw two adults and a small child, all in brown snowsuits, all with long branches masking-taped to their stocking caps. The woman stepped forward and extended her hand. "We're the Donaldsons," she said. "We're your neighbors."

"We're elks," the child added, touching the two branches on her hat. "These are our horns."

"They're antlers, sweetie," her mother corrected. "Bison and goats have horns. Elk have antlers."

Jean looked from the girl to her mother to the man beside them, who was calmly taking off his gloves.

"You're losing heat with the door open," he said, in a voice that was not deep so much as low and even. "You should probably let us in."

"Oh," Jean said, and she stepped aside so that they could pass. Then she shut the door behind her and leaned her back flat against it, touching it with her palms.

"Well, what's this?" the woman asked, kneeling next to Benny and picking up the photograph he'd dropped. "Is this a picture of you?"

"I'm sorry," Jean interrupted. "I'm terribly sorry, but I don't know who you are." The family in her cabin turned as one and looked at her.

"We're the Donaldsons," the woman said, frowning slightly, as if Jean's statement confused her. "We're your neighbors."

"We haven't got any neighbors," Jean said. "Not all the way out here."

"We just moved here today." The man spoke again in the odd low voice. The little girl was standing beside him, holding on to his leg, and he rested his hand on the top of her head, between her antlers.

"Moved where?" Jean asked.

"We bought an acre of land a half-mile from here." His tone suggested that he found her rude for pursuing the issue. "We're staying in our camper."

"Your camper?" Jean repeated. "I saw you today, didn't I? On the road?"

"Yes," the man said.

"You were driving awfully fast, don't you think?"

"Yes," he said.

"We were in a hurry to get here before dark," his wife added.

"You really have to be careful on these roads," Jean said. "It was very dangerous of you to drive that way."

There was no response; the three of them looked at Jean with politely empty faces, as if waiting for her to say something else, something perhaps more appropriate.

"I wasn't aware that there was land for sale at the end of our road," Jean said, and she was met with the same uniform expressions. Even Benny was watching her with a look of mild curiosity.

"We were not expecting to have neighbors," Jean continued. "Not all the way out here." Again, silence. There was nothing overtly unfriendly in their collective gaze, but it felt foreign to her, and she found it unsettling.

The little girl, who could not have been four years old, turned to Benny and asked, "What are you, anyway?"

He looked up quickly at Jean for an answer, and then back at the girl. Her mother smiled. "I think she wants to know what your costume is, dear."

"I'm a baseball player," Benny said.

"We're elks," the girl told him. "These are our antlers." She pronounced it *antlows*.

The woman turned her smile on Jean. Her teeth were wide and even, set close to her gums, like the teeth of those old

Eskimo women who spend their lives chewing on leather. "My name is Audrey," she said. "This is my husband, Lance, but he'd prefer it if you called him L.D. He doesn't like his real name. He thinks it sounds like a medical procedure. This is our daughter, Sophia. We threw these costumes together at the last minute, but she's very excited about them. She insisted that we trick-or-treat when she saw your cabin this afternoon."

"We were just on our way out," Jean said. "I'm taking Benny to his school's Halloween party."

"Isn't that fun?" Audrey beamed. "Are the little ones allowed to go?"

"No," Jean answered quickly, although she had no idea what the rules actually were.

"This will be our only stop tonight, then," Audrey said. "Though we may go for a walk later, to talk to the elk."

"Have you heard them?" L.D. asked.

"Excuse me?" Jean frowned.

"I say, have you heard the elk?"

"We hear elk all the time. I guess I'm not really sure what you're talking about."

L.D. and Audrey exchanged a brief look of shared triumph.

"L.D. is a musician," Audrey explained. "We vacationed here in Wyoming last summer, and he was very taken with the elk bugle. It's a wonderful noise, really."

Jean knew it well. Almost every night in the autumn, elk bugled across the woods to each other. It was impossible to tell how close they came to the cabin, but the sound was forceful and compelling: a long, almost primate screech, followed by a series of deep grunts. It was something she had known since childhood. She'd seen horses stop in the middle of a trail at the sound and stand there, heads pulled up high, breathing sharply out of their nostrils, ears tensed, listening, preparing to run.

"L.D. made several recordings. He found it very inspiring

for his own music," Audrey went on. "Have you ever lived in a city?"

"No," Jean said.

"Well." Audrey rolled her eyes. "Let me tell you, there's a limit, an absolute limit, to what you can endure there. Just three months ago, I was getting ready to go out on some errands and I suddenly realized I'd taken all my credit cards out of my purse so that, if I was mugged, I wouldn't have to go to the trouble of replacing them. Without even thinking, I'd done this, as if it was perfectly normal to live that way. And that night I told L.D., 'We're leaving; we have got to get out of this crazy city.' Of course, he was more than happy to comply."

Jean looked over to Benny, who had been standing quietly through all this, listening. She'd forgotten for a moment that he was there, and she felt the same quick guilt that came when, during dinner, she'd glance around the table and be surprised to see Benny eating with them, sitting between Ed and herself.

"Well." Jean pushed her glasses back farther on her nose. "We've got to get going."

"Listen," L.D. said, and he took a flat black disk from his pocket. He slid it into his mouth and made the full screech of an elk bugle ring through the small, heavily insulated living room of Jean's cabin. She saw Benny jump at the suddenness of the sound. L.D. took the disk out of his mouth and smiled.

"Oh, honey." Audrey winced. "That's so loud inside. You really shouldn't bugle in people's homes. Don't be scared," she told Benny. "It's just his elk talker."

Jean had heard one before. A friend of Ed's was a hunting guide who used one to call in bull elk. He'd demonstrated it for Jean once, and she'd laughed at how fake it had sounded. "You might as well stand in a clearing and call, 'Here elky, elky, elky,'" she'd said. L.D. had the same device, but his sound was full and alarmingly real.

Benny grinned at Jean. "Did you hear that?"

She nodded. "You do know that you can only hunt elk in season and with a license, don't you?" she asked L.D.

"We don't want to hunt them," Audrey said. "We just want to talk to them."

"Did it sound real to you?" L.D. asked. "I've been practicing."

"How'd you do that?" Benny asked. L.D. handed him the disk.

"They call this a diaphragm," L.D. explained, as Benny turned the object over in his hand and held it up to the light. "It's made of rubber, and you put it in the back of your mouth and blow air through it. It's not easy, and you have to be careful or you'll swallow it. There's different sizes for different sounds. This one is a mature bull, a mating call."

"Can I try it?"

"No," Jean said. "Don't put that in your mouth. It doesn't belong to you."

Benny reluctantly handed it back to L.D., who said, "Get your dad to buy you one of your own."

Jean cringed at the reference, but Benny only nodded, considering the suggestion. "Okay," he said. "Sure."

Jean took her coat off the hook by the door and put it on. "Come on, Ben," she said. "Time to go."

L.D. lifted Sophia from where she'd been sitting on his boots. One of her antlers had slipped from its masking-tape base and hung like a braid down her back.

"Doesn't she look precious?" Audrey asked.

Jean opened the door and held it so the Donaldsons could file out onto the porch. Benny followed behind them, small, antlerless. She turned the lights off and left, closing the door. She pulled a skeleton key from the bottom of her pocketbook, and, for the first time since she'd lived in the cabin, locked up.

It was a clear night, with a nearly full moon. There had been no snow yet, none that had lasted, but Jean suspected from the sharp smell of the cold air that there might be some by the next day. She remembered reading that bears wait until the first drifting snowfall to hibernate so that the tracks to their winter dens will be covered immediately. It was getting late in the year, she thought, and the local bears must be getting tired of waiting around for proper snow.

The Donaldsons were standing on the porch, looking past Jean's small back yard to the edge of the woods.

"Last summer I got the elk to answer," L.D. said. "That was a wild experience, communicating like that."

He slid the diaphragm into his mouth and called again, louder than he had in the cabin, a more powerful sound, Jean thought, than a human had a right to make around there, and disturbingly realistic.

Then there was silence, and they all stared across the yard, as if expecting the trees themselves to answer. Jean had forgotten her gloves. Her hands were cold, and she was anxious to get to the car, and warmth. She reached forward and touched Benny's shoulder.

"Let's go, honey," she said, but he laid his hand over hers in a surprisingly adult manner and whispered, "Wait," and then, "Listen."

She heard nothing. L.D. had set Sophia down, and now the whole family stood on the edge of the porch, their antlers outlined against the night sky. They'd best not make their costumes too authentic, Jean thought, or they'd get themselves shot. She pushed her fists down into the pockets of her coat and shivered.

After some time, L.D. repeated the call, a long high squeal, followed by several grunts. They all listened in the ensuing quiet, leaning forward slightly, heads tilted, as if they were afraid the answer might be faint enough to miss, although it was unnecessary to listen so carefully: if a bull elk was going to bugle back, they wouldn't have to strain to hear it.

L.D. sounded the call again, and immediately once more, and as the last grunt vanished into silence, Jean heard it. She heard it first. By the time the others tensed in realization, she'd already been thinking that it must be a bear making all that noise in the underbrush. And then she'd guessed what it was, just before the elk broke out of the woods. The ground was hard with cold, and his hooves beat in a light fast rhythm as he circled. He stopped in the black frozen soil of Jean's garden.

"Oh my God," she said under her breath, and quickly counted the points of his antlers, which spread in dark silhouette, blending with the branches and forms of the trees behind him. He had approached them fast and without warning, making himself fully visible to confront or to be confronted. Clearly, this elk did not want to talk to the Donaldsons. He wanted to know who was in his territory, calling for a mate. And now he stood, exposed, looking right at them. But the cabin was dark and shaded by the porch roof, so there was no way the elk could have picked out their figures. There was no breeze to carry a scent either, so he stared blindly at the precise spot from where the challenge had come.

Jean saw Sophia reach her hand up slowly and touch her father's leg, but, aside from that, there was no movement. After a moment, the elk stepped slowly to his left. He stopped, paused, returned to where he'd been standing, and stepped a few feet to his right. He showed both his sides in the process, keeping himself in full view, his gaze fixed on the porch. He did not toss his head as a horse might, nor did he strike a more aggressive, intimidating stance. Again he paced, to one side and to the other, slowly, deliberately.

Jean saw L.D. raise his hand to his mouth and adjust the diaphragm. She leaned forward and placed her hand on his forearm. He turned to look at her, and she mouthed the word *no*.

He frowned and turned away. She saw him begin to inhale,

and she tightened her hold on his arm and said, so softly that someone standing even three feet away would not have heard her, "Don't."

L.D. slipped the diaphragm out of his mouth. Jean relaxed. Out of the woods came two females, one fully mature, the other a lean yearling. They looked first at the male, then at the cabin, and slowly, almost self-consciously, walked the length of the yard to the garden. All three elk stood together for some time in what Jean felt was the most penetrating silence she had ever experienced. Under their sightless gaze, she felt as if she were involved in a séance that had been held in jest but had accidentally summoned a real ghost.

Eventually, the elk began their retreat. The older two appeared decisive, but the yearling twice looked back at the cabin, two long looks that Jean had no way of reading. The elk stepped into the woods and were immediately out of view. On the porch, no one moved until Sophia said very quietly, "Daddy."

Audrey turned and smiled at Jean, shaking her head slowly. "Have you ever," she asked, "in your entire life felt so incredibly privileged?"

Jean did not answer but took Benny by the hand and led him briskly to the car. She didn't look at the Donaldsons standing at the threshold of her home, not even as she waited for some time in the driveway for the engine to warm up.

"Did you see that?" Benny asked, his voice tight with wonder, but Jean did not answer him either.

She drove with only the low beams of her headlights on, recklessly, veering to the other side of the road, heedless of the possibility of oncoming traffic or other obstacles. She drove the road faster than she ever had before, venting a fury that took her four dangerous miles to isolate, and she did not begin to slow down until she realized that not only had she been manipulated, but she had been a participant in a manipulation. They had no right, she thought over and over, they had no right to do such a thing simply because they could. She remembered, then, that Benny was still with her, beside her, that he was entirely her responsibility, and she eased her car into control again.

She wished, briefly, that her husband was with her, a thought she immediately dismissed on the grounds that there were already far too many people around.

Alice to the East

* * *

T HE DRIVE from Roy's house to the center of Verona was
twenty minutes through sunflower fields that stretched
out on either side, flat and constant as a Midwestern accent. It was a good highway, well-paved and broken by nothing
but the horizon and the tracks of the Northern Pacific Railroad.
When Roy's daughter Emma was young, he had taught her
how to ride a bicycle on the yellow line that divided those who
were going east from those headed west. It was safe enough;
there was less traffic then, and the few cars that did pass could
be seen coming from miles away. There was always plenty of
time to make a decision, to move over, to be prepared.

About ten miles out of town the grain elevator could be seen,
standing with all the arrogance one would expect from the only
structure in the area over two stories tall. Roy had just passed
that point when he noticed an unfamiliar object ahead which
became, as he drove closer, a truck, a white truck, pulled off the
road, hazards flashing. He slowed down, read the Montana
license plate, and then eased his car so deliberately to a stop
behind the pickup that it appeared as if he'd parked there every
day of his life.

Roy stepped out of his car and walked a few feet before he saw them in the ditch. He stopped, and slowly reached out his hand until he was touching the hood over his warm, ticking engine. There were two of them, teenagers. The girl was standing. The boy knelt at her feet, slicing one leg of her jeans open at mid-thigh with a jackknife. Roy was startled and then embarrassed by the strange intimacy of the scene: the girl standing with her legs slightly spread, hands on her hips, the boy on his knees, the unexpected flash of the knife, the gradual revealing of more skin as a pair of jeans became shorts.

After a moment, the girl turned and looked at Roy with vague interest. Her hair, short and dark, was pressed damply against her head, as if she had just taken off a baseball hat. She wore a man's white undershirt, a pair of sunglasses clinging to its V neck with one arm.

"Hi," she said.

"I saw you were pulled over," Roy said. "I thought you might need a hand."

She gestured at the truck. "Yeah. It just quit on us all of a sudden."

"Fuel pump," the boy added. "Busted."

"Want me to take a look at it?"

The girl shrugged. "Just a sec," she said.

Roy waited while the boy cut through the last heavy inseam and the girl stepped out of the tube, with its hemmed bottom and frayed top. One leg bare, the other in long jeans, she walked to the pickup, opened the door, and released the hood. Roy came around to the front of the truck, noticing the dead butterflies and grasshoppers flattened against the radiator grill. He and the girl looked at the dusty engine block, and she pointed one thin hand through the network of tubes and hoses and said, "Pete thinks it's this that's broken. The fuel pump."

"If it is, you'll need a new one," Roy said.

"That's what Pete thinks, too."

"What is this, a three-fifty?"

"It's a Chevy," she answered.

"I mean the engine. What is it?"

"Three-fifty," the boy called from around the truck.

"I figured we'd have problems and everything," the girl said, "but damn. I thought we'd at least get through North Dakota."

"You're from Montana?"

"Yeah. Right across the border. Are you from here?"

"Yes," Roy answered. "I live just outside Verona." He thought it strange that he said this the way other people said they lived just outside Chicago or ten minutes from Manhattan. Like it meant something. There wasn't much inside Verona, and there was nothing just outside it, except sunflower fields and Roy's house.

"We haven't been on the road two days and now . . ." She left the thought unfinished and smiled at Roy. "I'm Alice," she said. With the *s* sound, the tip of her tongue made a brief appearance between her teeth and then vanished.

"I'm Roy. I know someone in Verona who might have the part you need. I can give you a ride. If you want."

"Let me ask Pete. My brother."

She walked back to the ditch, and Roy stood at the corner of the truck, watching. He didn't believe they were related. Something about the way she said "my brother" after Pete's name. Something about the emphasis, the hesitation.

Pete had been lying on his back in the dead grass, and at Alice's approach he sat up, wiped his forehead with the inside of his arm, and complained that it was hot.

"Finish making my shorts and he'll give us a ride into town," Alice said. "He told me some guy might have the part."

Pete took the jackknife from his pocket, opened it, and began to cut into what remained of Alice's jeans. Roy watched her stand there, still and relaxed, eyes forward. He saw that Pete, while bending his head in close concentration, did not touch Alice at all, not even brushing a knuckle against her skin. Only the frayed ends of her shorts grazed her thighs, and Roy found himself staring. He looked down at his own pants, studying the symmetrical cuffs that rested on the laces of his thick shoes.

When Pete finished, Alice stepped out of the second denim tube as she had the first, picked them both up, and draped them over her arm, like guest towels on a rack.

"Are you ready, Roy?" she asked, calling him easily by his first name.

"Sure." He nodded.

Pete stood up stiffly and brushed the dirt off his knees. "Let's go, then," he said.

Carl was behind the bar drinking coffee when they walked in. Roy asked if he'd seen Artie around, almost hoping that Carl would say no. It was cool and dark in the bar, and Roy didn't feel like hunting anyone down in the late-afternoon heat.

"His boys were just in for pops," Carl said. "They told me he was out back of his place cleaning snapping turtles. You need something?" Carl was looking at Pete and Alice.

"These folks had a breakdown about ten miles back. I thought maybe Artie'd have a fuel pump might work for them."

"Well, now, he might," Carl said. "If anyone'd have it, that'd be Artie." He glanced at Pete and Alice again. "You folks are lucky to break down here. Other places aren't so helpful."

"Well, then, how about a beer?" Pete said. "Alice? A beer?"

She shook her head.

"Just one, then. Whatever you got on tap."

Carl raised an eyebrow, and Roy knew he was wondering if the boy was under age. Roy didn't know how old Pete was and didn't really care, although he did wonder briefly how long it was since Carl had served a customer who was a stranger.

"I'll be back soon," Roy said, and left for Artie's.

There was one sidewalk in town, and he was halfway down it when Alice caught up to him.

"Hey," she said. "Mind if I come?"

Roy shook his head.

"This Artie guy have a shop or something?" she asked. "A garage?"

"No. Just a yard full of engines."

"What if he doesn't have it? The fuel pump."

"Then we'll have to drive to La Moure."

"Is that far?"

"Half-hour or so. Forty-five minutes, maybe."

Roy found himself picking up his pace to match Alice's, although it was too hot for anything faster than a stroll.

"That guy shouldn't've given Pete a beer."

"Carl? Why not?"

"Pete's only seventeen."

"Well. It's his bar."

"Still, he shouldn't sell Pete beer. The last thing I need is Pete drinking at four o'clock."

They walked, and Alice looked around, although there wasn't much to see. There wasn't a shop on the street that wasn't boarded up or closed, with the exception of Carl's bar and the post office. They didn't have a bank in Verona anymore. They didn't even have a grocery store.

When they reached Artie's house and Roy saw the front door lying across the porch next to a random pile of hubcaps, he began to wish that Alice had stayed back at Carl's with Pete. He didn't want her to think that everyone in Verona kept their property like that. One of Artie's boys ran out of the house and stopped when he saw Roy and Alice in the yard.

"Hi, Mr. Menning," he said. Roy smiled, but couldn't remember the child's name. There were three of them, all about the same age, all with homemade crewcuts and the hard, round bellies of kids who eat a lot but run around more.

"Is your dad around? Cleaning turtles?"

"He finished that this morning," the boy said. "Now he's fixing a chain saw."

Artie came from around the back, wiping his hands on his jeans, and, as if the front yard could only hold three at once, the boy vanished into the house. They were good kids, all three of them. Everyone said so. Terrified of their father, Roy had heard.

"I was wondering if you might have a fuel pump for a Chevy, a three-fifty," Roy said. "Some folks broke down out of town."

Artie was looking at Alice with interest. "What can I do for you?" he asked, as if Roy had not spoken. She seemed to understand the game, and asked for the fuel pump again. She didn't appear to be put off by Artie's long hair or by the tattoos that, like a lady's gloves, covered him from his hands to his elbows. Artie had left town as a teenager and returned for his father's funeral almost a decade later with the boys, the hair, the tattoos. Roy didn't like him, but he was the closest thing to a mechanic in town, now that the gas station was gone.

"Only Chevy parts I have are for that thing." Artie pointed at a small sedan without wheels resting on four pieces of firewood. The hood looked as if it hadn't been closed for years.

"You sure?" Roy said, but Artie ignored him, instead asking Alice where she was from.

"Montana."

"Where in Montana?"

"Fort Peck. Across the border."

"I know it," Artie said. "By the reservation."

"Yes."

"Shit. You're no squaw, are you?"

"No."

"I was gonna say. Better watch out for my scalp if you were, right?" Artie smiled, but it was an unnatural, almost painful, expression, as though he'd got a fishhook caught in one corner of his mouth, and someone was tugging at it.

"If you don't have the part, we're going to La Moure," Alice said, and Roy admired her for expressing the idea as if it were her own. As if she had the slightest idea where or what La Moure was.

"Not today, you ain't," Artie said. "Everything'll be closed by the time you get there."

Alice glanced at Roy, seeming to weaken with that piece of information. He noticed that Pete had cut her jeans unevenly, and the dingy gray cotton of her right pocket was showing about an inch below her shorts. It hung heavily, as if she were carrying a lot of change. Roy didn't like the idea of Artie being able to tell what was in Alice's pockets. He didn't like the way Artie watched Alice.

"We'll go to La Moure tomorrow, then," Roy said, and before Alice could answer, Artie said, "You look just like a girl I knew in Beaumont, Texas."

She looked at him, silent.

"You don't play the flute, do you?" he continued.

"No," she said, "I don't."

"Because this girl from Beaumont played the flute, is why I ask. You could be sisters. I wondered. What'd you say your last name was?"

"Zysk."

"Spelled?"

"Z-Y-S-K."

"Zysk." Artie whistled. "There's a word that'd bring you about a thousand points in a Scrabble game."

"Except it's not a real word," Alice said.

"Real enough for me," Artie said, and Roy decided that it was time to go right then. He thanked Artie, who asked, as they were leaving the yard, "Y'all up at Carl's?"

"We won't be for much longer," Roy answered.

"I'm gonna clean up and stop by."

"Like I said, we'll probably be gone by then."

"I'll see you there," Artie said, and stepped over a hubcap to enter his house through the screen door that guarded it so feebly.

Pete cursed at the news and told Roy, "We'll have to stay with you tonight."

"Goddamn it, you're rude," Alice said, and Pete walked to the other end of the bar to read the song list on the jukebox, which hadn't been plugged in since Carl bought the microwave.

"You're welcome to stay with me, you know," Roy said. "There's plenty of room."

"We'll stay in the truck. He's an idiot. He's a rude idiot."

Roy ordered a sandwich for Alice and a beer for himself. The bar was as quiet as a library.

"What do you do?" Alice asked.

"Me? I drive a snowplow in the winter and a combine in the summer."

"You're not a farmer?"

"Not anymore."

Carl brought Roy his beer and waved away his dollar, but Roy folded the bill and slid it under the napkin dispenser when Carl turned his back.

"Do you like those jobs?" Alice asked.

"Sure. I'm always finding people broke down when I'm snow-plowing."

Alice laughed. "You rescue them, too?"

"What I do is keep a stack of magazines with me."

"Why magazines?"

"I tell them to sit in their cars and read a magazine until help comes. Gives them something to do. Or else they get restless and decide to walk, and that's when they die."

"From walking."

"In the snow."

"From being bored. They die from being bored. Wow. If we'd started walking today, we just would've gotten hot."

"You're always better off staying with your car," Roy said, and Alice nodded.

"Are you married?" she asked.

"My wife died of a heart attack two years ago this winter."

Alice did not say that she was sorry, the way people usually did, so Roy did not have to say that it was okay, as he usually had to.

"I'm going to be a nurse," Alice said. "Maybe."

"That so?"

"Yeah. I'm going to Florida for nursing school. Pete's coming along with me to make sure I'm all right, and to work if I need money."

"That's nice."

"My mom made him go."

"Oh."

"You have kids?"

"One girl. She's thirty-two."

"She live around here?"

"She works in Minneapolis. She's a model, for catalogues and newspapers."

"She must be pretty."

"Yes."

"I'd like to do that, but my nose is too big."

"I don't know much about it."

"She must make a lot of money."

"Yes."

"She visit you a lot?"

"Not so much," Roy said. "Not since her mom died."

"I'll tell you what would be a great job," Alice said. "Photographer."

"I don't know much about that."

"Me neither." Alice looked behind her, at Pete and the jukebox, at the tall wooden cash register. "That Artie guy's a real piece of work," she said.

"I knew his father."

"He's a screw-up, huh?"

"I don't know."

"He reminds me of my brother. My oldest brother. With the tattoos and everything. All of my brothers are dumb, but this oldest one, I tell you, he's as good as retarded. Get this. When he was in the army in Germany, his girlfriend back home got pregnant. Here he's been gone five months and she's suddenly pregnant. So what she does is send him a letter saying, 'I miss you so much, I want to have your baby.' She says in the letter, 'If I had your baby, it would remind me of you and I wouldn't be so lonely.' What you have to realize here, Roy, is that my brother's wanted to marry this girl since forever. So she sends him a dirty magazine and an empty mustard jar and tells him to — I don't know how to say this — to do it in the jar and send it back to her so she can get pregnant with it. Understand?"

"Yes," Roy said.

"So my brother, a complete idiot, does this. And then he believes her when she writes to him and says she's having their baby. Can you believe that?"

"This was your oldest brother?" Roy asked.

"Yes. A fool. Everyone in the world knew about this scam, and people even told him that it was a scam, but he still believes her. *I* even told him that it was a scam, and he still believes her.

He still believes that it's their kid. Like whatever he sent from Germany to Montana made that baby after however many days in the mail."

Roy didn't know what to say, so he nodded.

"I'm sorry," Alice said. "That was gross."

"That's all right."

"But it shows how stupid my family is. My brothers, anyway."

"Well. That's some story."

"No kidding."

Artie walked into the bar. He had pulled his hair into a ponytail and was wearing a baseball cap, green, with a configuration of initials on it. His shirt had white snaps, and as he passed through a ray of sun they shone like dim, symmetrical pearls.

"Looks like you got some new company," he said to Carl as he sat down next to Alice. "Visitors from the distant land of Montana."

"Your kids were in today," Carl said.

"They causing trouble?"

"They told me you'd got yourself some snappers, is all."

"If my boys cause any trouble, you tell me."

"You better invite me over for soup," Carl said, and Artie asked Alice, "You like snappers?"

"Turtles? Never had them."

"Maybe I'll invite you over. You might like it."

Alice turned to Roy and said, "My next-to-oldest brother is Judd, and he's no genius, either. He took off, and for three years we never heard from him at all. Thought he was dead. Then one afternoon my mother gets a phone call —"

"She telling you her life story *already?*" Artie asked Roy, but Alice went on.

"She gets a phone call and it's from Judd. 'Hi, Mom,' he says, like he's been gone for just the afternoon. 'Hi, Mom. I'm in New Jersey at the recruitment center and the nice lady here says I can have three meals a day and new clothes if I sign up for the army. So, Mom,' Judd says, 'what's my Social Security number?'"

"What was it?" Artie asked.

"So Judd enlisted," Alice continued, ignoring him. "My mom says the army's the only refuge for dumb people like my brothers. If Pete wasn't going to Florida with me, he'd probably end up in the army, too."

"I been to Florida," Artie said. "I worked on a fishing boat there. I lived in a pink house. Right on the ocean."

"Really," Alice said.

Carl brought her a sandwich and she ate half of it before she spoke again. "My wisdom teeth are coming in. You ever get those?" she asked Roy.

"Yeah," Artie said. "Hurts like a bitch, but there can be no wisdom without pain." He laughed, one harsh burst, like an engine turning over in the cold, and then he asked Alice, "Why do you wear your hair short?"

"I like it this way," she said.

"Girls should have long hair."

"Boys should have short hair." She gestured at his ponytail.

"You got salt on your tongue, don't you?"

"I don't know what that means."

"You can be a wise-ass, is what it means," Artie said, and Pete was at the bar so fast that Roy realized he must have been standing behind them the whole time, waiting.

"Don't talk like that to my sister," Pete said.

Artie laughed again, that single, mechanical emission. "Billy the Kid here," he muttered. "Tough guy."

"Fuck you, pal," Pete said. "I said not to talk to my sister."

Roy heard Alice say, "Jesus Christ." She slid off her bar stool and edged out of the way, somehow anticipating what was coming. Roy's reflexes were not as swift. When Pete threw his punch and connected, he pushed Artie into Roy's shoulder, hard. Then Pete stood quiet and undefended while Artie got up, shook his head once, and squared his hat. With experienced precision, he swung and hit Pete in the center of his face and watched as he fell backward at a perfect diagonal, catching his head on the corner of the bar. The crack was louder than any noise heard in that room all afternoon, and then it was over.

To Roy's surprise, Alice approached him first, actually stepping over her brother to touch the sore spot on his shoulder where Artie had fallen.

"Are you okay?" she asked. Roy nodded.

"I'm sorry," she told him.

"Your brother should keep his mouth shut," Artie said.

"I wish you wouldn't talk to me." Alice's voice was low, and she wasn't even looking at Artie. "I really wish you would just leave me alone."

At this, Carl said, with no malice or heat, "You'll want to get home now, Art." He said it the way Roy's doctor a year before had said, "You'll want to stop eating salt soon." He said it the way Roy's wife used to tell Emma, "You'll want to have a warm coat with you this morning." A quiet command.

And Artie did leave, as if admonished by his own father, swearing under his breath but obedient.

Carl knelt by Pete and said, "He'll be okay. Just a bad bump is all."

"I'm really sorry," Alice repeated, and then she asked, "Could we take him somewhere, do you think?"

"We'll go to my house," Roy said. When he got up, he was surprised to find that his legs were shaking so much that he had to lean against the bar for a few moments before he could walk. The three of them lifted Pete and half-carried him out the door, down the steps, to Roy's car.

"Put him in the back seat," Roy instructed, and Alice said, "His nose, though. He'll get blood everywhere."

"That's okay."

As they slid Pete into the car, he opened his eyes for a moment, focused with difficulty on Alice's face, and said, "Mom told me —"

"Shut up, Pete. Will you please just shut your mouth?" Alice interrupted, and Roy thought that she might start crying, but she didn't.

"Got more than you bargained for, Roy." Carl laughed.

"I can't tell you how sorry I am about all this," Alice said again, but Roy only walked her to the passenger side and helped her into the car, as he had helped Pete.

They drove. West, out of Verona, the sun had just finished setting without ceremony, without color or effort. It was dusk, and still hot. Alice apologized again, and Roy told her that it wasn't her fault.

"All my brothers are idiots, all of them. My mom said I'm the only one in the family who could think my way out of a used tissue."

"How many brothers do you have?" Roy asked. The question sounded inane to him, considering the circumstances, but she answered immediately.

"Five," she said. "Steven, Lenny, Judd, Pete, Eddie."

"And you."

"And me. All of them are in the army but Pete and Eddie, who are too young. Eddie's only six. My brothers can't do a thing right."

They drove in silence through the sunflower fields. Roy thought to tell Alice that sunflowers always face east in the morning, west at dusk. He thought it might interest her, or even help her out, should she ever happen to get lost in North Dakota. She didn't seem to want to talk, though, so he kept it to himself. They passed the white truck, parked in a ditch, without commenting, and Alice spoke again.

"My littlest brother, Eddie, almost died last year," she said.

"He almost died. He was staying at our neighbor's house and it caught on fire. Everyone got out of the house but him, and when the fireman came into his room, Eddie hid under the bed. He got a glimpse of that oxygen mask and figured a monster was coming after him."

"That's too bad."

"It turned out fine. They found him and everything, and he was okay. But when they told me what happened, the first thing I thought was what a stupid kid my brother was, already. He's only six, I know, but to hide from a fireman in the middle of a fire . . . The thing is, if he'd died, I wouldn't've thought that he was stupid. I just would've missed him. There's a big difference, I guess, between almost dying and really dying."

Roy nearly said, *At your age you would think that,* but it sounded bitter even to him, so he didn't answer.

As he drove the familiar road, Roy thought about the empty, ruined homes of people he'd grown up with, people who were now gone: dead, or almost dead. Which Roy thought might very well be the same thing. Verona itself was almost dead, as well as countless other towns he'd known just like it. He thought about his wife, who had almost died twice before the final heart attack killed her. "I'm cold," his wife had said, having walked without shoes or a coat through the January snow to the garage, where Roy was refinishing their dining room table. "I'm cold," she said, and then she died, not almost, but really. Now Roy, with the bruised shoulder, with an unconscious boy in the back seat of the car he'd purchased for his wife, with a girl beside him half the age of his daughter, Roy felt as if he, too, were very close to death, almost dead.

As if she had been following his thoughts all along, Alice slid across the front seat and placed her hand over his. Her touch was at once that of a mother, a lover, a daughter, and it was so long since he'd known any of these things that Roy sighed, allowed his head to fall forward. He shut his eyes. Alice reached for the steering wheel, and he let her take it, knowing that the road was straight and safe, and that, for now, it would be better to let her steer.

"It's okay," she said, and reached under the wheel and turned on the headlights. It was not yet dark, but the lights would help them be seen by anyone driving east, or by anyone who might be watching their progress as they crossed the empty plains of North Dakota.

Bird Shot

◆　◆　◆

GASHOUSE JOHNSON came for Tanner Rogers just before noon. He knocked on the Rogerses' door and then waited, pacing the porch and examining the carpentry. His dog, Snipe, followed, limping like a man with a bullet in his spine. Tanner's mother, Diane, came to the door. She had all her pretty blond hair pulled back away from her face.

"Diane," he said.

"Gashouse."

"I want to take Tanner with me to the pigeon shoot today."

Diane raised her eyebrows. Gashouse waited for an answer, but she didn't give one.

"I think he'd like that," Gashouse said. "I think he'd like to see a pigeon shoot."

"He doesn't go," Diane said.

"I'd sure like to take him, though. On account of his father."

"He never went. Not with his father, either."

"What is that, Diane? A rule of your house or something?"

"It might be."

"Come on, Diane."

"I think it's a sick thing. I really do. I think pigeon shoots are sicker than hell."

"You used to love it."

"I never loved it. I never once loved it."

"You used to go."

"I did used to go. But I never loved it."

"Ed loved it."

"Tanner doesn't go," Diane said again. "He's not even interested in it."

"There are people up there who love Ed. A boy should meet the people who love his father. It's healthy for a boy to meet people like that."

Diane said nothing.

"I'm shooting for Ed today," Gashouse said. "Until they find someone else who can replace him permanently. Or until he gets better, I mean."

"That's very nice of you."

"I'm a good shot, Diane. I used to be a hell of a good shot when we were kids."

"Good."

"Of course, I'm no Ed."

"How many pigeons you plan on killing today?"

"Many." Gashouse smiled. "I'm going to kill so many goddamn pigeons. I'll see to it that Tanner kills a ton of pigeons, too."

Diane nodded, tired.

"Hell, I'll kill enough pigeons to make you a coat," he said, and then Diane did smile. Gashouse Johnson's smile widened. "How about it, Diane? Let me take your son up there and we'll bring you back a hell of a nice pigeon-fur coat."

Diane looked past Gashouse Johnson to Snipe, who was trying to lie down. "What happened to your dog?" she asked.

"He got old."

"He looks like hell. He looks like he got run over."

"He just got old."

"It's no place for dogs up there," Diane said. "Not for dogs or kids, either. Dogs get shot up there."

"No. Pigeons get shot up there. Nobody never shot a dog or a kid yet."

"Ed shot a dog up there once for chasing dropped birds."

"I don't know anything about that." Gashouse took out his handkerchief and blew his nose.

"Gashouse," she said, "do you want to come inside?"

"No, I won't bother you."

Snipe was lying down by a pair of boots near the porch steps, chewing on his tail. His head was thick and brown as a boot itself, and while he chewed, he watched Diane. His dog face was void.

"How old is he?" Diane asked.

"Eleven."

"Just the same age as my Tanner."

"I hope your boy is holding up a little better than my dog."

Diane smiled again. They looked at each other. After a moment, she asked, "Did you go see Ed in the hospital?"

"This morning."

"Did he tell you to come here and check on me? Is that it?"

"No."

"Did he tell you to spend some time with Tanner?"

"No."

"What'd he say?"

"Ed? He said, 'You think the first cigarette of the day tastes good? Wait 'til you try the first cigarette after a triple bypass.'"

This time Diane did not smile. "He told me that joke, too," she said. "Except that I don't smoke."

"Me neither. I chew."

"Well," Diane said, "I drink."

Gashouse looked down at his hands. Took a long look at his

thumbnail. Diane said, "You've got something on your beard. A crumb or something."

He wiped it off. He said, "Could've been toast."

"It looked like a piece of fluff."

"What's Tanner doing right now, Diane? Come on, Diane. Why don't you go ask your son if he wants to come along on a real live pigeon shoot?"

"You are an optimistic man, Gashouse. That's what you are."

"Come on, Diane. What's he doing right now?"

"Hiding from you."

"He'll love it," Gashouse said. "Unless he gets shot . . ."

"He might not even want to go, " Diane said, and Gashouse replied, "Ask him. Just go ask him."

Later, Tanner Rogers and Gashouse Johnson drove through town in Gashouse's truck. The boy was dressed in a heavy winter coat, a red hunting cap, lace-up boots. He was shy, and it took him some time to ask Gashouse the question he had been privately nursing.

"Isn't it against the law? To shoot pigeons?"

"Nah," Gashouse said. "Shooting pigeons is not against the law. *Betting* on people who shoot pigeons is against the law."

"What about my dad?"

"Your dad? Why, he doesn't bet. He just shoots the pigeons. Everyone bets on the shooters. You see? Everyone bets on your father, to guess how many pigeons he can shoot. Your dad don't need to bet."

"What about you?"

"I bet like a son of a bitch. What about you?"

Tanner shrugged.

"How much money do you have on you, son?"

Tanner took a handful of linty change from his pocket. "Dollar eighteen."

"Bet it all," Gashouse said. Then he laughed and yelled,

"Double it!" He slammed his hand on the steering wheel. "Double it! Triple it! Ha!"

Snipe barked once, a hound's low *woof.* Gashouse spun his head and looked at Tanner, suddenly serious. "You say something, boy?"

"No," Tanner said, "that was your dog."

Gashouse leaned forward and wiped the inside of the windshield with his sleeve. "Son," he said, "I was just kidding with you there. That was my dog barking. I knew that."

"Sure," Tanner said. "Me too."

"Good boy. We all had a little joke, right?"

"Sure," Tanner said. "Okay."

On their way out of town, Gashouse stopped at Miles Spivak's grocery store to buy shotgun shells. Miles himself was behind the counter, looking wintry and old. He found the shells that Gashouse asked for.

"Miles!" Gashouse shouted. "I'm shooting for Ed Rogers today. You should come on up there for once. You might have a good time, Miles! You might see some hell of a good shooting from me."

Miles took a slow look around his store, as if expecting to see another person appear behind him. "Damn it, Gashouse. You know I'm the only one here. You know I can't go."

"But I'm shooting today, Miles! Worth closing early for. I used to be a hell of a good shot."

Miles considered this.

"You know Ed's boy?" Gashouse put a big hand on Tanner's head.

"Have five boys myself. Just had the last one two months ago. By cesarean. You ever seen one of those?" Miles asked Tanner.

"For Christ sake, Miles," Gashouse said. "He's just a kid."

"Tied her tubes right there. So we won't have another kid. Now that's something to see, to see your own wife laid open like that. Women got some pretty tiny equipment inside. Ever seen those little things? Ever seen those little tubes?"

"Jesus Christ, Miles," Gashouse said. "Wouldn't you be surprised if the kid said yes?"

"Damnedest things," Miles said. "Tiniest, damnedest things you ever saw."

"Let's get out of here, Tanner," Gashouse said. "We got a crazy man!" As they walked to the door, Miles called after them, "She's a wonderful woman, my wife!"

"I'll tell you something about that one," Gashouse said when they were outside. "He's too dumb to bat both his eyes at the same time."

When they were back in the truck, Gashouse took the box of shotgun shells from his pocket and read the label carefully. "Hell," he said, "I don't know." He turned the box over and read it again.

Tanner waited, then asked, "What kind of gun do you have?"

"Twelve gauge." He looked over. "Does that mean anything to you?"

"My dad has a double-barreled eighteen gauge."

"Sixteen gauge," Gashouse corrected, putting the shell box back in his pocket. "Ed's got a double-barreled sixteen gauge. It's been a long time, son. I'll tell you that right up front. It's been a hell of a long time since I shot a gun."

Gashouse sighed, then slammed the steering wheel again. "Hey! But come on! It's not even my gun! It's Dick Clay's gun! Ha!"

Snipe woofed again from the floor.

"I didn't say anything," Tanner said.

"Ha!" Gashouse slapped his own knee. "Ha! You got the joke, son! You got it!"

Gashouse started up the truck and pulled out of the parking space. He said, "Good thing you like a joke, because we're on the road to big fun today, that's for sure. Any questions up there, you just ask me."

"Why do they call you Gashouse?" Tanner asked.

"Farts," he answered without hesitation. "Some real wood-chippers, too. Real ice-breakers. I'm better now, though, than I used to be. No more dairy."

"Does my dad call you that?"

"Yes."

"Does my mom call you that?"

"Tanner," Gashouse said, "it was kind of a consensus. You know what a consensus is?"

"No."

"Well," Gashouse said, "that's what it was."

At the next stop sign, Gashouse rolled down his window and yelled to a red-haired woman on the sidewalk, "Hey there! Hey there, you little stack of pancakes!"

She smiled and tossed out a wave as if it were a candy wrapper.

"Hey there! Hey there, you little side of fries! Hey there, you little deep-dish apple pie!"

The woman blew him a kiss and kept on walking.

"We'll see you later!" he yelled. "Cutie!"

Gashouse Johnson rolled up the window and said to Tanner, "There goes my girl. Can you believe she's fifty? Who would guess?"

"I think I know her from school," Tanner said, shyly.

"Possible," Gashouse said. "It is possible, because she does teach there sometimes on a substitute basis. She looks great, don't you think? A good-looking woman. You'd never guess her age, right? As long as she keeps her shirt on, right?"

Tanner flushed and leaned down to pat Snipe's head. The dog woke up and panted gratefully, his breath hot and ripe.

The man and the boy drove on, quietly. They drove out of

town and past the dump, past the cemetery, past the farms, past a cornfield with a fire engine parked beside it. The road became dirt, and they passed loudly over a cattle guard's wide grate. Gashouse drove farther still, up the forlorn road. He took a sudden left onto a mining road, driving slowly on deep ruts that might have been dug by tires, but might, too, have been dug by water. Where the wood line stopped abruptly, they came out at the edge of a wide, flat dish of rock and mud, the rough grave of an abandoned strip mine.

A few trucks were there already, lined up neatly, like cars at a drive-in. Men were talking in a small group, kicking at rocks, their dogs milling around beside their muddy feet. Gashouse and Tanner got out of the truck. Snipe followed, painfully.

"Hey!" Gashouse said to Dick Clay. "Place your bets!"

"Can't," Dick said. "No birds. Willis got shut down."

"By who? By the hell who?"

"By . . ." Dick hesitated. "By the authorities."

"Well," Gashouse said. "Don't I just feel like a slapped butt?"

"Happens." Dick shrugged.

"Not in twenty years, it hasn't happened," Gashouse said. "Willis got shut down by the authorities, did he? Son of a bitch. By *what* goddamn authorities?"

The other men looked at one another . One of them coughed and said, "Just some officers of the law doing their job."

"Just some good old boys," another man said. "Just some fellas enforcing the law, for once."

"It's not against the law to shoot pigeons," Tanner said.

The men looked at him.

"Gashouse?" Dick Clay asked quietly. "Is that Ed Rogers's boy?"

"Sure is." Gashouse again put his big hand on Tanner's head.

"Ed don't want his boy up here, Gashouse," Dick said.

"That's not true, Dick. It's *Diane* who don't want the boy up here."

"What'd you do? Kidnap him?"

"I invited him," Gashouse said. "I invited him to come up here and watch me stand in for his old man. I invited him to come up here and watch me shoot some birds for his old man."

The men looked at one another, looked at their boots, looked at their dogs.

"I came here to shoot some pigeons, and by Christ, I'll shoot them," Gashouse said. "I'm calling up Willis. I aim to find out what the hell's going on. See what this is all about. Authorities shutting him down. See if I can't do something about it."

"Actually," Dick said, "actually, it doesn't really matter. Nobody's planning on showing up anyhow. On account of Ed being in the hospital. The pigeon shoots are pretty much canceled for now."

"But *I'm* shooting for Ed," Gashouse said, and smiled, as if he'd solved something. "*I'm* shooting for Ed, and any folks who normally bet on Ed Rogers, why, they can bet on me."

Dick said nothing.

"For Christ sake, Dick. You know I'm shooting today. You lent me your goddamn gun, Dick."

"I got to tell you something," Dick said, "because you're my good friend. The truth is, Gashouse, the authorities didn't shut down Willis. That's the truth, Gashouse."

A few of the men started heading back to their trucks, in a sort of casual way.

"Dick?" Gashouse said. "Where the hell are people going?"

"Gashouse," Dick said, "I will say this. And I'm only telling you what I've been hearing. This is not me talking. This is what the guys are saying. I told some guys that you wanted to shoot for Ed, and some guys said they would rather cancel the shoot. Some guys don't think that a bet on you is much of a bet. Some guys think they might just want to stay home until we find someone else."

The men stood quietly then, like mourners or surveyors.

"Well," Gashouse said finally. "Well, well, well. We won't fault anyone for that. Will we, Tanner? Will we, son?"

In Willis Lister's barn, there were dozens of pigeons. The pigeons were caged, sitting in the dust of old feathers and shit. The sound of all those birds was a collective gurgle, like something thick about to come to a boil.

"Dick Clay told me not to show up," Willis Lister was explaining to Gashouse Johnson. "On account of Ed. He told me they were canceling the pigeon shoots for a while."

"See, now," Gashouse said, "I realize that. But I thought Tanner here might want to see me shoot for his dad. Tanner's dad is in the hospital, you know."

"I know that."

"And I thought it might be a special thing for the kid to see a pigeon shoot. On account of the high esteem that all the guys have for his old man. I thought he might want to see me shoot some birds for his old man. On account of the high esteem I have for his dad. And the high esteem that I have for his mother."

The pigeon man squatted down and looked at Tanner. "I'm sorry," he said, "about your father." Willis was an old man. Still, his face was smooth and unmarked, except for a small scar the shape of a sickle, pink against his cheek and shiny as a fleck of mica.

"Thank the man." Gashouse nudged Tanner.

"Thank you," Tanner said.

Willis stayed squatting. "Son," he said, "your hair is really kicking today." He took a comb from the bib pocket of his coveralls and offered it.

"I'm okay," Tanner said.

Willis kept looking at him, waiting.

Tanner said, "I already combed it today."

"It's really kicking, though. A boy should try to keep himself neat."

"I went to sleep on it last night and it was wet. I can't fix it."

But Willis still held out the comb. Gashouse nudged Tanner once again. "Why don't you use the man's comb, son?"

Tanner took the comb from Willis Lister's hand and ran it through his hair once. Then he handed it back.

Gashouse said, "Why don't you thank the man for his offer of a comb?"

"Thank you, sir."

"You're welcome, son," Willis said. "Don't you look neater now?"

Willis stood up and faced Gashouse. "What do you need here?"

"Birds."

"Nobody's up there to bet, Gashouse. There ain't gonna be no shooting today."

"Don't need betters," Gashouse said, grinning. "I just need birds. I'll shoot them right here."

Willis didn't answer, and Gashouse stamped his foot and laughed loud enough to send the pigeons into a boil of talk. "Hey! I mean — not *here!* I'm not going to shoot your pigeons *here* in their damn cages. The boy didn't come here to see me shoot birds in a cage! I'll shoot a few of them in your yard. Just so the boy gets an idea." He stopped laughing, found the handkerchief in his pocket, and blew his nose. Willis looked at him and also at Tanner, who was patting down his hair with both hands. Willis looked at Snipe, who was licking the wire door of an empty birdcage.

"How many?" Willis asked. "How many birds for your little venture?"

Gashouse returned the handkerchief to his pocket and pulled out a wallet, from which he took a twenty-dollar bill. "Can you give me four birds for twenty dollars? Can you do that, Willis?"

Willis looked pained. "Four birds? What's four birds? I lose more birds than that to rats in a week." He turned to Tanner. "How many pigeons you want to kill, son?"

"Me?" Tanner looked nervously to Gashouse.

"I'm shooting, Willis," Gashouse said. "I'll explain it to you again. Point is, I want the boy to see how his dad does it. Want the boy to see how his dad got so famous."

"How many birds?" Willis asked.

"I only need to kill one, I guess."

"Hell, Gashouse, you can *have* one bird. What the hell is one bird to me?"

Gashouse looked at his thumbnail carefully. "Problem is, it might take me a few birds to kill one . . ."

"Christ, man."

"Come on now, Willis. It's been a long damn time. I might miss the first bird or so." He paused. "You know, I used to be a hell of a good damn shot when —"

"You can have three birds," Willis interrupted.

"I used to be a hell of a shot."

"You can hit one bird in three, can't you?"

"My God," Gashouse said. "We'd all better hope the hell so."

Willis went to the nearest cage, stepping over Snipe, who was still licking at a wire door as if it were gravy. He opened the trap and pulled out the birds one at a time — by a foot, by a wing — with a frown at the dust and down raised from the panic. He tucked a pigeon under each arm like a schoolbook and handed a third to Tanner. "Tuck his wings down," Willis instructed, "so he don't beat the hell out of himself."

Tanner followed the men out of the barn, carefully carrying the bird away from his body, as though it were something that might spill on him. He waited in the field with Willis while Gashouse went to the truck for his shotgun. Snipe sat in front of Willis Lister, looking hopefully at his pigeons.

"What do you think, dog?" Willis said. "You think I got a biscuit for you?"

Then they were quiet. Tanner was miserably uneasy to be alone with Willis Lister. The grass in the yard was high, thick to the middle of Tanner's shins, and damp. There was the kind of gray sky that can mean rain any minute or no rain for months. Tanner's pigeon was hot and thick, bigger than the cradle of his two hands. Beside him, Willis breathed heavily from his mouth, like a deep sleeper, and after a long time said, in a low voice, "You think I got a biscuit for you, dog? That what you think?"

Gashouse Johnson came back with the shotgun and shells. He knelt in the grass to load, and Willis said, "What the hell kind of shells you using? You planning on shooting bear out here?"

Gashouse looked at the box and did not answer.

"That's not bird shot, man. You hit a bird with that stuff, you'll be lucky to find the goddamn thing. You'll blow the thing all to bits."

Gashouse loaded the shotgun and stood up.

"You really planning on shooting those hand grenades?" Willis asked.

"You know," Gashouse said, "I honestly don't care what kind of shells these are. I think I'd just like to kill these birds and go on home." He held the gun to his shoulder, waiting.

"You know what boys like you do up at the pigeon shoots?" Willis said to Tanner. "There's always a job up there for a boy your age. You think you can do a boy's job?"

"Sure," Tanner guessed.

"This is the boy's job. You wait for the shooter to drop the bird out of the sky. Then you chase that bird down, and if it ain't dead, you kill it off. Just a neck-wring'll do it. You think you can do that easy job?"

Tanner looked at the fat bird in his hands.

"That's a boy's job," Willis said. "Okay. Get behind the man, son, lest he blows your goddamn head off with his lousy shooting."

Tanner backed up.

"Okay," Willis said, "let's go."

Willis pulled one of the pigeons from under his arm and tossed it into the air. It fluttered low, over their heads.

"Wait, now," Willis told Gashouse. "Let her get some height."

The bird flew. It flew out and away from them, straight toward the trees at the end of the field. Gashouse shot once, a tremendous blast that knocked him over backward, almost into Tanner. The bird flew on, into the trees. Willis, still holding the second pigeon in his hands, looked at Gashouse, who was sitting in the tall wet grass, rubbing his shoulder.

"Okay," Willis said. "Ready?"

"That gun's a kicker," Gashouse said. "Knock a guy right on his ass."

"It's the shells," Willis said. "Plant yourself better. Ready?"

Gashouse stood and raised his gun. Willis tossed the second bird up, and it flew in the same line as the first had.

"Now!" Willis shouted.

Gashouse shot, missed, shot again, missed again. They watched the pigeon make it to the line of trees and vanish. Snipe lay at Tanner's feet, groaning unhappily from the blasts of noise. Willis Lister stared out toward the end of the field.

"Let me ask you something," Gashouse said. "Now, will those birds of yours eventually come back to your barn? Eventually? I don't want you to lose two good birds for nothing."

Willis turned to Tanner. "When I tell you, I want you to toss that pigeon of yours up in the air. Not too hard. Ready? Now! Now!"

Tanner opened his hands and raised them. The bird shifted slightly but stayed put.

"Go," he whispered.

Tanner jerked his hands, and the pigeon tumbled forward and out of his palms. It flew briefly, then settled on a rock in front of Willis Lister.

"Shoo!" Willis waved his hat at the bird. "Shoo!"

The bird flew a few feet and landed in the grass. Willis swore and picked it up. "Sick bird," he said, and handed it to Tanner. "Go get another one. Leave this one in an empty cage."

Tanner walked back to the barn with the wet, heavy bird. He found an empty cage. The bird, when dropped inside, stayed where it fell, facing away from Tanner. He shut the wire door, which was still damp from Snipe's mouth. In the other cages, the pigeons moved around, stepping and nudging one another for better positions. He found the cage with the fewest birds and, reaching in slowly, caught one by the foot. It fluttered horribly, and he dropped it. He shut his eyes, reached in again, grabbed a wing, and pulled the pigeon out. He ran with the flapping body tucked under his jacket, as if he had stolen it and was being chased.

Gashouse Johnson and Willis Lister watched him coming, and when he was before them, Gashouse said, "Good boy," and Willis took the bird.

"Ready?" Willis said, and tossed the pigeon up and away from them. It circled, then flew.

"Now," Willis said. "Now!"

Gashouse shot once, and the bird dropped. Straight to the grass. Snipe took off after the bird and found it more or less accidentally, by running over it. The pigeon was still alive. It had not fallen far from them. They walked over to it, quickly. It had lost a wing.

"Get it," Willis Lister said. Not to Gashouse. Not to Snipe. But to Tanner.

"Go on, get it," he said. "Just a neck-wring'll take care of it."

Tanner did not answer or move.

Gashouse said, "Now your *father*, he could drop twenty birds in a row, just like that. How about that, son?"

"Jesus Christ," Willis Lister said, and squatted beside the bird. He lifted it just enough to get his hands around its neck and twist, and as he was doing this, the bird made one twist of its own — a small adjustment toward comfort or resistance — and died. Willis dropped the bird on the ground.

"Stay the hell off that thing," he said to Snipe, and wiped his hands on his coveralls.

They walked back to the truck.

Gashouse said, "If I'd have missed that last bird, I was going to start aiming at the side of the damn barn. See if I could hit the side of a goddamn barn! Ha!"

"Careful of the gun," Willis said sharply to Gashouse. "Don't go blowing your goddamn leg off like an idiot."

"Time was, I used to be a hell of a good shot." Gashouse laughed. "Of course, that was twenty-odd years ago. Could be I might've been piss awful then, too, and just forgot about it. Ha!"

Willis Lister spoke to Tanner without looking at him. "At a pigeon shoot," he said evenly, "when a man brings a bird down, it is always a boy who wrings the neck."

Tanner nodded.

"That's a boy's job," Willis said. "Always has been a boy's job."

"You want to go for a beer?" Gashouse Johnson asked Willis.

"No."

"What about you, Tanner? You want a soda pop?"

"Take the boy home," Willis said. "Nobody wants any soda pop neither."

The dress that Diane Rogers had been wearing that morning was hanging over the kitchen sink, just washed, when Gashouse Johnson returned with Tanner. It was a thick cotton dress and it dripped steadily onto the dishes below, like something melting. She had changed into slacks. She watched as Gashouse sat at the table, Snipe at his feet.

"Tell your mother what a crack shot I am," Gashouse said to Tanner.

"Crack *pot*," Diane corrected.

"Come on, Diane. It was something to see."

"Did you win any money?"

"I wasn't betting. I was shooting."

"I was asking Tanner."

"I wasn't betting," Tanner said.

"Good for you."

"Nobody was betting," Gashouse said. "Nobody was even there. On account of respect for Ed." Gashouse leaned forward and pointed at Diane. "Out of *respect*. They canceled it out of respect for the man."

They looked at each other gravely. Then Diane laughed. She went to the refrigerator and got beers for herself and Gashouse. She got a glass of juice for Tanner.

"How bad a shot are you, anyhow?" she asked.

"I'm a fine shot. We got our shots in."

"Where?"

"Willis Lister gave us three birds."

"Four," Tanner said.

"Okay." Gashouse shrugged. "We shot at four birds."

"Three," Tanner said. "One was too sick."

"Just for kicks, you were shooting?" Diane asked.

"So that your son could see what his father does."

"One bird died," Tanner said.

Gashouse opened his beer, twisting the cap off with a corner of his shirt over his palm. He put the cap in his pocket.

"Diane? You ever tell Tanner that Willis Lister is your cousin?"

"No," she said. "When I was little, my mother used to say,

'Don't let your cousin Willis kiss you. You tell me if he tries to touch you.'"

"That's not true."

"Honey," Diane said, "you were absolutely not there."

"Could have been."

"I don't want to talk about Willis Lister."

"Tanner?" Gashouse said. "Did I ever tell you that your mother was the first girl I ever kissed?"

"No," Diane said. "And don't tell him that again, either."

"Ha!" Gashouse laughed, and slammed the table so hard that Tanner's juice quivered in its glass.

"You have a girlfriend these days?" Diane asked. "Some poor little thing?"

"Yes, I do."

"Blond?"

"Brown."

"Brown?"

"Brown hair."

"Blue eyes?"

"Brown."

"Well. That's not your normal taste, Gashouse."

"Brown skin, too."

"How about that?"

"She's pretty much brown."

"Well." Diane took a long drink of beer. "Sounds beautiful." They both laughed.

"She's okay," Gashouse said. "She's no you."

"Neither am I, anymore. Not these days. I'm too old."

"That's not true. That's a damn lie. It's always nice to sit with you, Diane. It always has been nice to sit with you."

"Hm," Diane said. "Saved up any money?"

"Five thousand bucks in the bank."

"As we speak?"

"Just sitting there."

"You owed Ed about that much just last winter."

"Yes, I did."

"I don't know. Seems to me, a man who owes five thousand dollars one minute and has five thousand dollars the next minute hasn't really saved that money. He just hasn't spent it yet."

"Maybe," Gashouse said.

"Don't spend it all on that girl."

"Come on, Diane."

"I know you."

"I should hope the hell so."

"She call you Gashouse?"

"She calls me Leonard. Lee-oh-nard . . ." Gashouse drawled in three long syllables.

"How old is she?"

"Twenty," Gashouse said without blinking. When Diane didn't answer, he added, "Turning twenty-one next week."

Gashouse waited, then said, "Next Thursday, as a matter of fact. Yes, sir. The big two-one."

Diane tucked one of her feet under her body and asked, "What's her name, Gashouse?"

There was a beat.

"Donna," he said.

Diane did not respond.

"Having a big party for her, actually," Gashouse went on. "For her and her friends. Her little school friends. Hell, you know how girls are."

"Gashouse," Diane said kindly. "All your lies are safe with me."

"Diane —" he said, but she cut him off with a slight and elegant wave. An authority of silence.

They did not speak. Young Tanner Rogers had been sitting with one foot on his chair all this time, and he had untied the lace of his wet boot. He was practicing knots with the short length of damp rawhide lace. It was too short a lace for complicated knots, but he was repeating smoothly a simple knot of three steps — a rabbit around a tree and down a hole, a quick, snug pull. Diane looked at her son's hands, working. She got up for a paring knife, and when she sat down, she laid her own hand on the table, palm up.

"Give me that dirty paw," she said.

Tanner gave his right hand to his mother. She gripped it in all confidence. With her paring knife, she dug under his thumbnail just firmly enough (shy of the pink bed of skin) to pull up a thin, crumbling line of brown dirt. She wiped the knife on her knee, then cleaned the next nail and the next and the next. Gashouse Johnson watched. And Tanner watched, too, sitting still, with his left hand hovering over the knot he had made — a sportsman's knot, a modest knot — that will hold and hold, but can release, too, with a quick tug, in emergencies or at the end of its usefulness.

Tall Folks

* * *

I N THE GOOD, good days when the Ruddy Nut Hut was across the street from the Tall Folks Tavern, there was a steady passage of drunks from one place to the other, every night. It was as if the two bars were one bar, weirdly split by the four fast lanes of First Avenue.

Ellen owned the Tall Folks Tavern, and the Ruddy Nut Hut was her husband Tommy's. They had been married for fifteen years, separated for thirteen, hadn't slept together in two, and held no particular interest in the politics of divorce. Tommy was a fabulous drunk. It was impossible to get kicked out of his bar — not for fighting or falling down, not for being broke or under age. Tommy delivered every possible permission. Ellen delivered famous bartenders. Not all of her bartenders were great beauties, but several were. The others had their own specialized appeal, such as immediate sympathy, great wit, or reassuring alcoholism. Ellen always kept one bartender who was good with names, as a guarantor of hospitality, and she always kept one mean bartender, because there are people who crave that, too. There are people who crave a mean girl who calls fat guys "slim" and throws ugly drunks out by hand. If it was not somehow possible to fall in love with a girl in five minutes,

Ellen would not hire her. She had done very well this way, brokering these particular and necessary loves. And Tommy, too, had done very well.

The Ruddy Nut Hut had pinball and darts. The Tall Folks Tavern had a pool table. Some nights, one place had toilet paper or cigarettes when the other did not. And in the hot summers, the drunks crossed that stretch of First Avenue as if it was someone's back yard, as if the moving cars were harmless as swing sets or sandboxes, as if the twin bars were just neighbors' picnics, welcome as any suburb.

Then Tommy didn't pay his rent for eight months, and the Ruddy Nut Hut closed. All that autumn, Ellen's customers left their drinks and stepped out of the bar for air, paced, stepped back inside again quickly, restless and irritated.

In December, the Ruddy Nut reopened with a hand-lettered banner that said WALTER'S TOPLESS. The front window had been painted black, and a sign hanging in it said, "The most beautiful ladies in the world." On the door was a smaller sign that said, "The world's most beautiful ladies," and the final, smallest sign, which was really just a note, explained that Walter's Topless would be open every day of the week. At noon.

Ellen had a nephew named Al. She had hired him to be her plumber, which meant that he was in charge of digging rotting lemon wedges out of the sink drains, and replacing the toilets that the young men sometimes tore out of the bathroom walls to commemorate great moments at the pool table. Al was nice to look at and easy to talk with. If he had been a girl, he would have been a perfect Tall Folks Tavern bartender. He would have been the kind of pretty that union guys are crazy for, and Ellen would have given him the Thursday evening happy hour shift. If Al had been a girl working Thursday happy hours, the carpenters and teamsters would have come in every week and tipped the hell out of him for being so pretty. After Tommy left, Ellen spent most of her time with Al, and it was Al who went with her when she finally crossed the street to check out Walter's Topless.

Ellen knew everyone drinking at the bar when she walked in that night.

"These are all my people," she said to Al.

"And Tommy's."

"Tommy can't really claim any of these people anymore, can he?"

It still looked like the Ruddy Nut Hut, except that the pinball machines were gone, replaced by a small stage with a wide mirror behind it and a long rail in front. There was one stripper dancing — a skinny girl with knees wider than thighs and a druggie rock star's tiny hips. Ellen knew her, too.

"That's Amber the junkie," she said.

Amber smiled over at Al, and shook her chest at him. Her breasts were just nipples on a rib cage. Al smiled back.

"She's terrifying," he said.

"She used to come into my bar and drink rum and Coke all day," Ellen said. "I used to try to catch her shooting up in the bathroom, but every time I'd go in there she'd just be brushing her teeth."

"That's almost grosser."

"Almost."

"You should put blue lights in the bathrooms. That's what they do in fast food places. Then the junkies can't see their veins and they can't shoot up."

"That's a little bit mean, I think."

"I like blue lights," Al said. "In a blue-lit room I can't see my balls."

"Stop that," Ellen said. "That's not true."

There was a girl behind the bar in a dark bathing suit. Ellen didn't know her. She had black hair with a serious center part, and the bathing suit was a practical one-piece, faded, with tired elastic and wide straps.

"She looks like she should be wearing flip-flops," Al said.

There was a man behind the bar with her, and when he turned to face them, Ellen said, "Walter?"

He was carrying a case of beer, which he brought over and set on the bar in front of Al. He had a long beard, seedy and gray, like the beards of prophets or the homeless.

"Hello, Helen," he said.

"Ellen," she corrected. Walter said nothing.

"Don't even tell me this is your bar now, Walter."

Walter still said nothing.

"What the hell are you doing with a place like this? Nobody told me this was your place."

"Sign tells it."

"I didn't know you were the Walter."

"What else Walter is there?"

"I'm Al," Al introduced himself. "I'm Ellen's nephew."

The two men shook hands over the case of beer between them.

"Walter?" Ellen said. "I'm not sure about the name of this place. You should at least call it Walter's Topless *Bar*. Walter's Topless sounds like an announcement. It sounds like you're the one that's topless."

"It is an announcement."

"I guess so." Ellen looked around. "Tommy didn't tell me he'd sold it to you."

"It's me."

"I'm just surprised."

"I don't know how come. Sign says it plain enough."

"Walter?" Ellen said. "Secretly, I always thought you were Amish."

Al laughed, and Ellen laughed, too.

"I'll buy you a drink on the house," Walter said. "And one for your nephew."

"Thank you, sir," Al said.

"We'll take two beers and some good Scotch," Ellen said. "Thanks."

Walter took two bottles from the case and pulled an opener out from inside his shirt, where it hung on a chain, like a heavy crucifix. He opened the beers, which were just short of cold, and put them in front of Al and Ellen.

Walter went to the end of the bar for the Scotch and Al said, "I haven't called anyone 'sir' since I was twelve."

"Walter can't run a strip joint," Ellen hissed. "He hates women. He never even used to come to my bar, because he hated women bartending. Jesus Christ, what a lousy joke."

Walter came back with two shots of Scotch. Ellen drank hers and left the glass upside down on the bar. Al smelled his and set it in front of him carefully.

"Who's your bartender?" Ellen asked.

"Rose," Walter said. "My daughter."

Walter and Ellen stared at each other in silence.

"Wow," Al said. "I was thinking of asking for a job, but she's probably staying, I guess."

"I have three daughters," Walter said, still looking at Ellen. "They all work here."

"Are you going to drink that?" She asked Al, and when he shook his head, she put back his Scotch, too, and set the glass next to her own. "This is the funniest thing, Walter," she said. "It's so funny that Tommy didn't tell me it was you. But good luck and everything, right?" Ellen took a twenty-dollar bill out of her pocket and slid it under her beer bottle. "Make sure Rose keeps us happy down here," she said, and Walter walked away.

On the stage, Amber the junkie was finished. She was sitting on the floor, buttoning up a man's long-sleeved shirt. She looked as tiny as a third-grader. Walter changed the tape and adjusted the volume, and another girl came up out of the basement and onto the stage. She had red hair in a braid from the top of her head, and without a lot of performance, she took off her bra and started bobbing lightly on her toes, as if warming up for a jog.

"We can't compete with all this tit," Ellen said.

"Sure we can."

"This is such dumb stuff. Why should anyone cross the street for this stuff?"

"They won't," Al said.

"But if it's just plain old tit they want, we can't compete with that."

"Polly takes her shirt off sometimes," Al said.

"Yeah, but only when she's really drunk. Then she cries and everyone feels bad. It's not the same thing as this. Plus, Polly only works on Monday nights."

"You're right."

"What if Walter tries to hire my bartenders to dance here?"

"They won't."

"If someone could get Polly to take off her shirt and look like she was enjoying it . . . that would be something, wouldn't it?"

"A guy would pay for that," Al said.

Ellen waved to a huge man as he walked in, and he came over and sat beside her.

"Wide Dennis," she said. "Good to see you."

Wide Dennis kissed Ellen and ordered a beer for himself and a Scotch for her. She patted his head and smiled. Wide Dennis had a head thick and faded as an old buoy. He had far-apart eyes that tended to lean randomly and outward, as if he were watching every corner at every time. He smelled like baby powder and spit, but he was smart enough to do something with computers that perhaps only two other people in the world could do, and he was paid well for this.

"Did you know this was Walter's place now?" Ellen asked him.

"Just found out."

"I always thought he was Amish," Ellen said.

"I always thought he had a friend in Jesus," Wide Dennis said.

Ellen laughed. "Remember Willy? Walter's brother?"

Wide Dennis rolled his eyes.

Ellen said, "Willy could put his whole fist in his mouth, remember?"

"He put his whole damn near fist in my mouth a few times."

"I don't know that guy," Al said.

"You'd know him if you saw him," Wide Dennis said. "He'll be the guy banging someone's head against a Dumpster. Talking real loud."

"He was a hell of a talker," Ellen said. "Listening to Willy tell a story was like getting stuck behind the school bus. If anyone was going to open a damn strip joint in that family, it would be that bastard Willy, not Walter."

Wide Dennis took a dollar bill from his pile of change and went up to the stage. He handed the dollar to the red-headed dancer. He said something to her as she took it, and she laughed. Ellen ordered two more beers, and when Rose brought the bottles over, Ellen asked, "What do they say to those girls, usually, when they give them money like that?"

Rose shrugged and walked away.

"Can't shut that girl up," Ellen said. "Just like her Uncle Willy."

"Usually they tell her she's beautiful," Al said. "They tell her she's a great dancer or something."

"That's sweet."

"You used to strip. You remember how it is."

"Not in a place like this," Ellen said. "Not professionally. Just in the beginning, at Tall Folks. Just to get people in there." Ellen drank her Scotch. "It worked; that's the truth. Some of those people still haven't left. Actually, some of those people are in here right now. Can't remember anyone ever handing me any money for it, though."

"How's my boy Tommy been doing?" someone behind Al asked. Ellen looked around her nephew and smiled.

"Hello, James."

"Hello, Ellie."

"Where've you been, James? We miss you."

James waved at the stage. There was another dancer up there now, a tall black girl who was swaying, with her eyes shut. They all watched her for a while. She swayed and swayed, slowly, as if she'd forgotten where she was, as if she thought maybe she was alone. They watched her for some time and she didn't do anything more than sway, but nobody was in any hurry to look at anything else. The redheaded girl gathered up her things and crossed the stage behind the swayer.

"Oh, my," James said. "Will you look at that?"

"Which one?" Al asked.

"All of them! Everywhere!" James smiled. He had a front tooth missing, from where Tommy had fallen down on him one night and James had hit the floor with his mouth.

"Do they let you sing here?" Ellen asked.

James shook his head. He used to come to the Tall Folks Tavern and stand under the light by the cigarette machine to sing. Ellen would turn down the jukebox and threaten the circus into some kind of silence, and they would all listen to James. He used to dress for it, too, in a found suit, dress socks, and sandals. He looked like Nat King Cole but sang better. The light above the cigarette machine shadowed his face just right. People used to cry. Even sober people used to cry.

"How's my Tommy doing?" James asked again.

"He's so fat now you wouldn't believe it."

"Always was a big man."

"Now he looks like a monk. Drinks like a fish, still."

"Like a monkfish," Al said, and James laughed and hugged him. James was wearing a leatherish coat that looked as if it had been made out of pieces of car seats. Patches of brown and gray and darker brown.

"I do miss Tommy," James said.

"And we miss you," Ellen said. "Stop over. Make the time."

James nodded toward the swayer on the stage.

"We've still got girls across the street, honey," Ellen said.

James did not even nod this time, and Ellen whispered into Al's ear, "I want my people back." He squeezed her hand.

Ellen got up and went to the bathroom, which looked the same as it always had. Above the urinal, it still said, "I fucked your mother," and in a different pen below it said, "Go home, Dad. You're drunk."

Ellen put on lipstick and washed her hands without soap or paper towels, which she was used to. Under the mirror was the oldest piece of graffiti in the place, a decade-long joke. "Top Three Things We Like Most About Tommy," it said. "#1) He's not here." There were no listings under numbers two and three.

"Ha," Ellen said out loud.

She stayed in the bathroom a long time, ignoring a few quiet knocks and one quick pounding at the door. When she finally came out, the dark-haired girl with the serious center part was standing there. They smiled at each other.

"Rose," Ellen said.

"I'm Sandy. Rose is my sister."

"You look like sisters."

"We all work here."

"I heard that. It's like a cottage industry. It's like a bodega," Ellen said, and when Sandy did not answer, she added, "I'm Ellen."

"I know."

The two women looked at each other. Sandy was wearing a bathing suit like Rose's, but she had shorts on.

"How's business?"

"Great," Sandy said. "And you?"

"Great," Ellen lied.

"Good." Sandy smiled. "That's real good."

"Are you waiting for the bathroom?"

"I'm just sort of standing here."

"Do you know my nephew Al?" Ellen pointed down the bar. "He's the cutest boy here."

"He sure is," Sandy said.

"He told me the other day that he's been in love with me since I used to push him around in his baby carriage."

"Wow."

"Do people fall in love with the girls in this bar?"

"I don't know. Probably."

"I don't think they do," Ellen said. "I think they just like to watch."

"I don't guess it matters," Sandy said.

"Your dad doesn't even like girls. Excuse me for saying it."

"He likes us."

"You and your sisters?"

"Yes."

"Does he like Amber the junkie?"

Sandy laughed.

"Don't laugh at Amber. She's a sweetheart. She's from Florida, poor kid . . . It's hard to say," Ellen said. "I used to have this bartender, Catherine, who had this walk. People used to come to my bar on her shifts just to watch her walk back and forth. Not your father. He never liked my bar."

"Do you like his bar?" Sandy asked, and she smiled as she asked this.

"See, Sandy. It's like this," Ellen said. "Not really. You know?"

"Sure," Sandy said. "I think I'll go in there now." She pointed to the bathroom, and Ellen moved out of her way.

"Sure," Ellen said.

Ellen made her way back to Al and ordered more Scotch for both of them. Wide Dennis was still there, and James in his car-seat coat was there, too, talking to Amber the junkie.

"I don't like this place," Ellen said to Al. "Who's going to come to a place like this?"

"Me, neither," Amber said. She was eating a sandwich out of one of those small coolers people use for carrying around six-packs or organs fresh for transplants. She was drinking what could have been a rum and Coke. "This place is the worst."

"Nobody loves anyone here," Ellen said, and Al took her hand and squeezed it. She kissed his neck.

"He's the sweetest boy," Amber said.

"Remember that bartender you used to have over there? Victoria?" James asked Ellen. "She was a sassy thing, that girl."

"She worked Wednesday nights," Al said.

"She worked Tuesday nights, baby," James said. "Trust me please on this one."

"You're right." Al nodded. "It was Tuesday."

"My God, I do miss that girl."

"She was a good bartender," Ellen said.

"Those were good, good times. We used to call that the Victorian Era, didn't we? When Victoria was still working."

"That's right, James."

"Get that girl back again. That's what we all need."

"Can't do it."

"Tall Folks was holy back then. We used to drink out of that damn girl's hands."

"She has kids in grammar school now," Ellen said.

"They don't make girls like that anymore. That's the truth."

"They're always making girls like that," Ellen said. "They just keep on making them, and there's one of them across the street at my bar right now, if you're craving a great girl."

"Who?" Al asked. "Maddy? Not Maddy. Hardly."

"I don't drink like this all the time," Amber the junkie said suddenly. "You know that? Some days I don't drink for two weeks."

Then they were all quiet, looking at Amber.

"Okay, sweetie," Ellen said. "That's great. Good girl."

"Sure," Amber said. "No problem."

Behind the bar, Walter was changing the cassette again, and a new dancer stepped up onto the stage.

"Wow," Al said.

"I know, baby," James said. "You don't have to tell me."

She was blond but not a born blond, with dark eyebrows and short hair, combed down straight against a round, round face. She wore fishnet stockings and garters, big clunky 1940s high heels, and a short antique pink dressing gown that tied in the front. She was chewing gum, and as the music started, she looked down at Al and blew a bubble.

"Jesus Christ," he said.

"That girl is a pin-up," Wide Dennis said.

She danced for a while with her robe on, then slid it off and coyly folded it at her feet. She stood up to face the bar with naked breasts, and her nipples were perfect and tiny, like some kind of cake decoration.

"She's beautiful," Ellen whispered to Al.

"Ellen," he said, "I would eat that girl up with a spoon. I really would."

"She's a steamed dumpling, isn't she?" Ellen said.

The dumpling had an actual act. She worked the bubble gum and the stockings and her flushed little arms. She worked the big clunky shoes and the belly and thighs. She held every available attention.

"You know what I feel like?" Ellen asked Al. "I feel like I'm looking at a pastry, you know? In a bakery window?"

"Yum," Al said gravely. "Yum."

"You could melt cheese on that girl."

"You know those tubes of biscuit dough you can buy in the dairy case?" Al asked. "You know how you smack them on the counter and they go *pop* and all the dough pops out?"

"Yeah."

"She came out of one of those tubes."

The dumpling was dancing in front of the mirror, looking at herself. She put her hands against the reflection of her own hands and kissed the reflection of her own mouth.

"That's what strip joints are all about," Wide Dennis said. "Greasy mirrors."

"You know what she's leaving on that mirror?" Al said. "Butter."

"That's not lipstick she has on," Ellen said. "That's frosting."

Al laughed and pulled Ellen tight, and she put her arm around his shoulders.

"You should give her some money," he said.

"No way."

"It'll be cute. I'll go with you. She'll like it. She'll think we're a married couple and our therapist told us to come here so we could have better sex."

"She'll wonder how I tricked a twenty-year-old into marrying me."

Ellen put her face against Al's neck, which was warm and salty. Wide Dennis went up to the stage and leaned his huge self against the rail, as if he were on a veranda or a cruise ship, as if the scenery were delightful and vast, as if he were a man of great leisure. He pulled dollar bills out of his pocket one at a time and held them up suavely between his second and third fingers. The dumpling accepted the money somehow within her choreography, and managed to tuck each dollar bill into her garter as though it were a slip of paper with a phone number on it that she thoroughly intended to call later. Against Wide Dennis, she looked slightly miniaturized, a perfect scale model of herself.

"He'll stand there as long as he has money, won't he?" Ellen asked.

"She's the sweetest girl," Amber the junkie said. "I love her."

The dumpling leaned down and took Wide Dennis's huge head in her hands. She kissed him once over each eyebrow.

"I love that girl," James said.

"Me, too," Al said.

"I love her," Ellen said. "I love her, too."

Ellen drank the last of her Scotch and said, "This is bad news for me. This place is really bad news, isn't it?" She smiled at Al, and he kissed her with his boozy, pretty mouth. It was more of a kiss than aunts usually get. He kissed her as if he had been planning the kiss for some time, and Ellen called up all of the lessons of her considerable history to accept and return it with grace. She let him hold the back of her head in one reassuring hand, as if she were a weak-necked baby, feeding. To Ellen, his mouth tasted like her own fine Scotch, nicely warmed.

When Ellen and Al finally crossed back over to the Tall Folks Tavern, it was closing time, and Maddy the mean bartender was kicking out her last drunks.

"Go home!" she was yelling. "Go home and apologize to your wives!"

Ellen did not ask Maddy how the night had been and she did not greet any of her customers, but walked behind the bar and picked up the lost-and-found box. Then she and Al went together to the back room. Ellen spread the lost-and-found coats over the pool table. Al turned off the low overhead light, and the two of them climbed up onto the pool table, with its thin mattress of other people's clothes. Ellen stretched out on her back with a damp jacket pillow and Al settled his head on her chest. She kissed his smoky hair. In the dark of the back room, without a window or a fan, the air smelled like cigarette ashes and the dust of chalk. It smelled something like a school.

Much later, more than an hour later, Al did roll carefully on top of Ellen, and she did lace her fingers snugly against his back, but before this they rested for a long time, still in the dark, holding hands like old people. They listened to Maddy the mean bartender throw the last drunks out of the Tall Folks Tavern, and they listened to her clean up and shut down the bar. On the best nights, Ellen used to dance on that same bar with her arms spread open wide, saying, "My people! My people!" while the men crowded at her feet like dogs or students. They used to beg her not to close. It would be daylight and they would still be coming in from across the street, begging her not to close. She told this to Al, and he nodded. In the dark of that big back room, she felt his little nod.

Landing

◆ ◆ ◆

I LIVED in San Francisco for three months and only slept
with one person, a redneck from Tennessee. I could have
done that back home and saved myself a lot of rent money.
A city full of educated, successful men, and I went after the first
guy I saw wearing a John Deere hat.

I noticed him at the bar because he looked out of context
among all the businessmen, sitting there in his plaid shirt and
white socks. He was drinking a beer and I saw a can of chewing
tobacco beside the bottle. If there's one thing I hate, it's a man
who chews tobacco. I sat down next to him.

"What's your name?" I asked.

"You sure made a beeline for me," he said.

"That's a hell of a long name," I said. I ordered a beer and
settled onto the bar stool. He told me that he was Dean.

"I'm Julie," I said. "What are you doing in San Francisco,
Dean?"

"Uncle Sam stationed me here."

I thought, I didn't come all the way to California to pick up
some enlisted guy in a bar. I thought, I didn't come all the way
out to California to pick up some good old boy with a cheap

watch and a crewcut, some yokel from a town probably smaller than my own.

"So, what is it exactly that you do in the army, Dean?"

"I jump out of airplanes." Something about his drawl made the comment sound drenched with innuendo. He looked at me appraisingly; there was a long pause.

"Well," I said, finally. "That must be fun."

Dean kept his eyes on mine for a moment. He unfolded the paper napkin in front of me, held it over my head, and let it go: a tiny parachute with "Pierce Street Bar" printed on a corner. The napkin fluttered down and settled on my pack of cigarettes.

"You fall and fall," he said. "And then you land."

I took a long drink and put the bottle down evenly on its own damp ring. I had started feeling that magnet pull at the back of my knees and the gentle tug just under my stomach.

"Do you have cowboy boots?" I asked him.

"Why?"

"Because I'm not crazy about those shoes you're wearing. You look stupid with white socks and dress shoes. I think you'd look a whole lot better with cowboy boots coming out from those jeans."

Dean laughed. "Sure, I got cowboy boots. Come back to the Presidio with me tonight, I'll put them on for you."

"You don't throw away much time buttering up a girl with conversation, do you?" I asked, and wrapped my hand around my beer bottle. Dean covered my hand with his.

"You sure got nice hands," he said.

"I was just going to take a drink," I said, and I thought my voice sounded a little bit too low and shaky. I cleared my throat.

We looked at his hand on mine and at my hand on the bottle, and I said, "You've got nice hands, too. Big, but nice." I could feel his calluses against my knuckles. "You know what they say about men with big hands," I continued, and Dean grinned.

Landing

"What's that?"

"Big gloves."

It was easy to find Dean's truck. It was the only pickup with Tennessee plates on Pierce Street, and it was right across from the bar.

"You drove this thing all the way to California?"

"Yup. Only took me two days."

There was an empty doughnut box on the front seat, and the passenger side window was stuck at half-mast. Plastic six-pack rings, fast food bags, and empty cassette boxes covered the floor, and I felt something crack under my foot as I got in.

"What was that?" Dean asked, and I read the label on the box.

"Hank Williams Junior's Greatest Hits Volume Two. You're kidding me."

"What's the matter, never heard country music before?"

"I wish."

Dean started up the truck and pulled off Pierce Street.

"Where'd you say you were from, Julie?"

"Main Street," I said. "USA."

"You got some South in your voice."

"Maybe."

"Scoot over here," Dean said, patting a spot next to him. I slid over, close as I could get. "I want to put my arm around you," he said, "but I have to shift."

I took his hand off the chipped black ball on top of the gear shift and put his arm around me.

"We driving all the way to the army base in second?" he asked.

"I'll shift," I said, and that's how we drove: me shifting, my other hand on his left thigh so I could tell when he was pushing the clutch, my face near his chest so I could feel him breathing and see the snaps on his shirt. Dean drove with his hand on my shoulder and then under my arm against my ribs, and finally at my breast.

We were quiet for some time, and then Dean said, "Talk to me. Tell me something."

I put my mouth against his ear and slid my hand up his thigh. He shut his eyes.

"Keep your eyes on the road," I whispered, and he smiled and opened them. I could see the pulse in his neck.

"Your bed narrow or wide?" I asked, and, quietly, Dean said, "Narrow."

"I think that I want to see you in these jeans, all faded, with cowboy boots coming out from the bottom of them," I said. "I want to lie on your bed and see you standing there with no shirt, just those jeans down low on your hips and cowboy boots. Just looking at me. Okay?"

Eyes forward, Dean swallowed and nodded. I kissed his ear.

"I think you'd look great like that," I said.

I woke up the next morning to see a guy with white-blond hair and camouflage pants walking around, stepping over the tangled pile of my shirt, bra, and skirt. He had a mole on his left cheek the size and color of a BB.

Dean and I had fallen asleep back to front, my spine cushioned against his chest and stomach, my hair in his face and mouth.

"Dean?" the stranger called, looking at me. "You up?"

"Hey, Hunt," Dean said into the back of my neck.

"Who's the girl?"

"This is Julie. Julie, this is Hunt. My roommate."

"Hey," I said.

Hunt the roommate didn't answer, so we looked at each other some more. He had a long cleft in the middle of his chin, another miniature cleft at the tip of his nose, and a deep furrow between his eyes. It looked like someone had made markings in preparation to cleave his face in half, but had never got around to finishing up.

Under the scratchy green army blanket, Dean slid his hand flat between my thighs. He let it rest there, cool and immobile but full of possibilities.

"Where'd you sleep last night, Hunt?" he asked.

"TV lounge."

"No way."

"Way."

"You didn't have to do that, man." Dean moved his hand up higher between my legs.

Hunt grinned, but only on one side of his face, like a stroke victim. "I came by 'round three this morning," he said, "and I heard you two rockin', so I didn't come knockin'."

Dean laughed. I turned over in the bed, careful to keep myself covered, and faced him.

"I'm not crazy about your roommate," I whispered in his ear, and he laughed harder.

"Julie don't like you, Hunt," he said.

"I just seen that Madonna video," Hunt said, unmoved by Dean's remark. "You know that one where she's in that man's suit, grabbing her twat like Michael Jackson does?"

"Yeah, I know it," Dean said.

"She's hot, huh?"

"Uh-huh."

I tried to get my head comfortable on Dean's chest, somewhere away from his collarbone, and traced the silky thin track of hair under his belly button with my finger.

"I'm gone watch some more TV," Hunt told us. "Maybe they'll show it again. They been playing it a lot."

"Uh-huh," Dean said.

"If I come back, y'all want me to knock?"

"Up to you, man."

As soon as Hunt was out the door, Dean was on top of me, pulling my thighs up around his hips. I locked my fingers behind his head.

"Oh, baby," Dean said, "I'm so glad we're awake again."

"So, you don't like my roommate?" Dean asked. We were parked in his truck at the far end of Baker's Beach, drinking beer, watching the only two people in the water toss a Frisbee back and forth.

"When they drown, we can have the beach to ourselves," I said.

Dean's truck smelled like the burgers we'd just finished.

"They can have the beach," Dean said. "Too damn cold to swim, anyhow. I'm happy we got the parking lot." He stuck his little finger into the neck of his beer bottle and swung it slowly in front of his face, as if trying to hypnotize himself. "I got my finger stuck one time doing this."

"That's a pretty smart thing to do, then, isn't it?"

He pulled his finger out with a pop and held it up. I leaned over and bit it.

"Taste like beer?" he asked.

"Not really."

Dean pulled me close and ran his tongue across my lips, lightly. "I like the way you taste."

I kissed him, then sat back against the seat. "No, I don't like your roommate," I said. I put my feet up on the dashboard and looked between them at the swimmers. "Where's he from, anyhow? Alabama?"

"West Virginia."

"Yeah? Well, I don't like him. He reminds me of guys from my town. I know what he's all about."

"That right?"

"Uh-huh." I combed the hairs on Dean's leg back the wrong way with my fingertips and smoothed them down again. He was wearing shorts, no shirt. Cowboy boots. "Hunt's got a truck with six-foot wheels, I bet," I said. "Got a belt buckle that says 'The South Will Rise Again.' Someday he'll get a girl pregnant, maybe his cousin, and they'll have more kids just like him. Bunch of kids running around with ringworm, eating mud pies."

Dean laughed. "So what kind of guy do you like?" He balanced his beer bottle on the palm of his hand.

"College boys," I said. "Lawyers. You know."

Dean nodded, interested. "Let me ask you something. You hooked up with a lot of guys like that since you left home?"

I looked at him evenly. "All I said is that's the kind of guy I'm attracted to."

He nodded again. "So you aren't attracted to guys like me?"

"No, I'm not."

Dean set his bottle on the dashboard and gently pushed me down so that I was lying on my back, flat on the seat.

"I didn't think so," he said, and slid my underwear out from under my skirt, past my ankles, off. He pushed my skirt up around my waist, put his head between my legs, and started to kiss the insides of my thighs.

"I really fucking love that," I said after a few minutes, and Dean looked up.

"You got some mouth for a girl supposed to be from the country."

"You've got some mouth yourself," I said.

It was midnight at the International House of Pancakes.

"Happy anniversary," Dean said, and toasted me with his milk shake. "We been together a whole day."

"These waitresses aren't so great," I said, and lifted my water glass, not for a toast, but for a refill. "I've been sucking on this ice for a half-hour now."

"Ten minutes," Dean corrected me.

"Well, anyhow. A waitress should look after stuff like that. A good waitress."

"When you smile, the bottom part of your eyes look like this." Dean dipped his finger into his milk shake and drew a half-moon shape on the tabletop. "I like that."

The skin around my mouth felt sore and raw from Dean's stubble, and it hurt to sit down from all the sex. Dean leaned his head against the turquoise vinyl seat and shut his eyes.

"You worn out yet?" I asked, and he smiled and shook his head without opening his eyes to the fluorescent lights.

"No, sir. I'm all set for another round."

"Liar. I saw you walking like a cowboy before."

"It's the cowboy boots make me walk like that."

The waitress filled my water glass and we didn't speak for a while. Then I drank the water in one swallow, cleared my throat, and said, "Well . . . it's sure been nice knowing you, Dean."

He lifted his head from the back of the seat and looked at me with eyes the amber color of whiskey aging at the bottom of a barrel.

"You going somewhere?" he asked.

"Not really. Or, maybe yes. I may stay in San Francisco, but I could leave soon, too. I don't like staying anywhere too long, you know?"

Dean didn't answer, waited.

"Or maybe I'll head down to L.A.," I continued, shifting my eyes from Dean's face to study first the dessert case, then the restroom doors. "I've also been thinking about going up to Seattle, or maybe Portland."

"You planning on leaving tomorrow or something?" Dean looked puzzled. I rolled my eyes.

"Look, I don't want to fight about this."

"Nobody's fighting nobody. I just wondered what you meant about 'nice knowing you.'"

"Dean, you're a nice guy and everything, okay? But I'm not looking for any kind of relationship. I don't want to see you getting attached to me or anything."

"What?"

"That's not what I came all the way out here for."

"Yeah?"

"Yeah."

I reached for a bottle of maple syrup. I turned it upside down and watched the brown fluid move inside, slow as lava.

"You and me don't have anything in common, Dean. You're going to finish with the army, then head back to Tennessee, probably. That's fine; that's great for you. But that's not for me. I'm not going to end up married in Tennessee."

"I don't remember asking."

"You know what I mean."

"No, I don't."

I reached across the table for his hand, and he let me take it, the way you let a waitress take an empty plate.

"Dean," I said, "listen. Two thousand miles is a long way to go for something you can get next door. Okay?"

He didn't answer right away. His voice was not accusing when he finally said, "Plenty of guys at the Pierce Street Bar got what you're looking for, Julie. If that's what you want, what'd you sit next to me for?"

I took my hand off his and put it in my lap. I looked down at my sleeve, dirty from the floor of Dean's room.

"I know what you're all about . . ." I started to say, wanting to sound as level as Dean, but trailing off.

"No, you don't, Julie. You don't half know me."

"Well. I think I do."

"You're making a mistake to think that," he said. "You don't know me at all, hardly, and you're making a mistake to think otherwise."

We looked at each other across the table. Dean's face was

even and open. I didn't come all the way out to California for this, I thought, but I didn't say anything.

I watched as a waitress at the dessert case sliced a tall white cake and slid a wedge carefully onto a plate. She glanced behind her, then licked a smear of frosting off her thumb. Another waitress was scrubbing the inside of the large coffee urn with what appeared to be a toilet brush.

"What're you doing?" Dean asked after some time.

"Nothing," I answered. "Watching."

He smiled slightly.

"What?" I said.

"Nothing." Dean's smile widened. "It's just that I don't see you jumping up and running off."

"You think I won't?"

Dean shrugged. "I'm just waiting, is all."

"Okay," I said. "Okay."

The waitresses moved through the restaurant, seating customers, serving food, sliding tips into their apron pockets. Someone came out of the kitchen with a mop to clean up a spill. The manager worked on a crossword puzzle and sipped from a tall glass of milk. I watched them, and Dean sat quietly across the table, waiting.

I thought, How long is this guy going to sit here?

But Dean did not get up to leave, and neither did I.

Come and Fetch
These Stupid Kids

◆ ◆ ◆

MARGIE AND PEG were arrested after they got drunk on the chef's cooking wine and went into the parking lot and rubbed butter on the windshield of every car parked there. It was late at night. It was also late in September, and long past the end of the tourist season. There had been very few customers that evening, in the restaurant where Margie and Peg worked, and there were very few cars in the parking lot. As it happened, though, one of the cars that Margie and Peg buttered turned out to be the police car of a Delaware state patrolman. They hadn't noticed that it was a police car. They hadn't really been paying attention. The Delaware state patrolman came out of the restaurant and into the parking lot, where he handily caught the girls in the act of vandalism.

Peg started to run when she saw him, but Margie shouted, "Don't run, Peg! He'll gun you down like a dog!"

Which Peg believed, although the Delaware state patrolman had done nothing more threatening than bark, "Hey!"

The patrolman held Peg and Margie in the parking lot and radioed for a town cop to come and deal with the situation.

"Come and fetch these stupid kids," he told the town cop over the radio.

The Delaware state patrolman stood in the parking lot with Margie and Peg, waiting for the town cop. It rained and rained on them. The patrolman was wearing a practical raincoat, but the girls were soaked in their waitress uniforms.

"I wonder if we might be allowed to go *inside* the restaurant while waiting for the other policeman to arrive," Margie requested. "I wonder if it might not be more pleasant *not* to stand in the rain as we await the arrival of that gentleman. No?"

Margie had a habit (newly developed that summer) of speaking in such an aristocratic and refined manner. A very new habit. A very new affectation, which was not enjoyed by every individual she encountered. On this night in particular, Margie sounded as if she were coming very close to calling the Delaware state patrolman "my good fellow." The Delaware state patrolman looked at Margie, in her wet waitress uniform, talking so archly. Margie was clearly drunk. Margie had one eyebrow raised inquisitively. She had one finger pressed coyly against her chin.

"You can stand outside in the rain all night, for all I care, Little Miss Du Pont," the Delaware state patrolman said.

"That's very funny," Peg told him.

"Thank you," he said.

The town cop showed up. He looked bored. He was so bored, in fact, that he charged Margie and Peg with public drunkenness, disturbing the peace, and vandalism.

"Gracious!" Margie said. "That is quite a lot of serious charges for a harmless little prank such as our own."

The girls were loaded into the town cop's car and taken to the local jail, where they were fingerprinted and booked.

Peg's boyfriend, a handsome guy named J.J., eventually arrived to bail out Peg and Margie, but not before the two girls had spent a few hours in the tidy jail cell.

"Take a look around you, ladies," the bored town cop had said when he was locking them up. "Get a feel for it. Remember what it feels like to be behind bars. Not so nice, is it? Remember that feeling, next time you decide to commit a crime."

Margie and Peg took a look around. They got a feel for it. They chewed some gum that Margie had, and then fell asleep. When Peg's boyfriend J.J. finally showed up to spring them out of jail, it was already three o'clock in the morning.

"You two are turkeys," J.J. said, and he brought the car around to the front of the station so the girls wouldn't get any wetter.

They drove home. The rain was hitting the car hard, hail-like. Each drop of rain had the weight, it seemed, of an un-cooked bean. The Delaware shore was getting just a small piece of some hurricane farther out in the Atlantic, but it was a dramatic piece.

J.J. drove with his chin almost touching the steering wheel, trying to see the road. Peg slept in the back seat. Margie found some gum that was stuck in her hair and worked it out.

"The cop told me you two were supposed to spend the whole night in jail, but I talked him out of it," J.J. told Margie.

"How did you manage to accomplish that, you clever darling?" Margie asked.

"I told him that the road to our house might be washed out by morning from all this rain, and I might not be able to come and get you. He was nice about it."

"Men certainly do like to talk about manly things like roads being washed out, don't they?"

"That's right," said J.J.

"Did you give him a firm and manly handshake, J.J.?"

"Yes, I did."

"Did you call him sir?"

"Yes, ma'am."

"Good for you, J.J.," said Margie. "Thank you so very much for releasing us from that dreadful prison."

When they got back to the house, Margie's spoiled and foolish boyfriend John was awake.

"I demand to have a drink with the criminal masterminds," John said.

John had the same habit that Margie had, of speaking in a refined and aristocratic manner. Actually, Margie had inherited her speech pattern directly from John. John had invented it.

"Do you think we are loathsome, John?" Margie asked, and kissed him on the cheek.

John said, "I have a demand! I demand that we sit outside in this magnificent rain and hear chilling tales about life in the big house."

Margie said, "Foolish John. Silly John. Don't you realize that *this* is the big house?"

Margie was absolutely right. It was a very big house, indeed. It was John's house. He was only twenty-one years old, but he owned this big house right on the Delaware shore. His parents had given it to him as a graduation present. Margie's parents, by contrast, had given her a bracelet. Peg's parents had taken her out to dinner for a graduation present, and J.J.'s parents had sent him a graduation card, signed by all his aunts and uncles.

John was rich. His father was a producer who lived in Hollywood and was very rich. As for John's mother, she was a former Miss Delaware. She was divorced from John's father and lived in a mansion on Chesapeake Bay. She had driven down only once that summer to visit her son at his new beach house. She had arrived in a Mercedes, and that car had looked as black and hard as a wet rock.

John planned to live in his graduation gift house on the beach forever, and he had invited his friends from college to live with him just as long as they wanted. Originally, there had been five young people living there, in John's house. They'd had only two names between them. There had been three Margarets and two

Johns. Some had nicknames, and some did not. They were John, J.J., Margie, Mags, and Peg.

"Gracious!" John had observed with delight. "We are a full house. We consist of a pair and three of a kind. Isn't that lucky? Isn't that a marvelous hand to be dealt?"

But Mags left the beach house at the end of August and moved to Florida.

Mags secretly said to Peg, "I'll tell you something, Peg. The fact is, I'm beginning to hate John."

John said about Mags, after she had gone, "She was welcome to leave at any time. Nobody has to stay in this house simply to please me. Although she might have thought to replace herself with another Margaret, just to keep up our lucky hand of cards, no? Alas! Now we are merely two pairs. But you will all stay, won't you?"

"We will all stay!" Peg had said, and hugged her handsome boyfriend J.J.

"Is the house even winterized?" J.J. had asked John.

"Oh, mercy! I don't know," said the spoiled and foolish John. "Couldn't you winterize it, J.J.? You're so clever. No? How hard could that be, to winterize my house?"

In fact, the house was not winterized, as its four occupants were beginning to realize by the end of September. They did not have any realistic way of staying warm. What's more, by the night of Margie's and Peg's arrest, it did not even appear that any of the four young people had a job. J.J.'s job as a lifeguard had ended right after Labor Day, when the tourists left. It certainly seemed that Margie and Peg would be fired from their waitressing jobs, after their drunken butter prank in the parking lot of the restaurant. As for spoiled and foolish John, he'd never had any sort of job whatsoever. John had passed his summer growing his hair and writing sequels to movies that already had sequels.

"Well, my resplendent jailbirds," said John. "Let us commence to the roof. Let us sit upon the widow's walk and drink some alcohol while enjoying this magnificent rain."

So it passed that the four friends climbed up onto the roof of John's big beach house to drink some beer and watch the weather. They were just a dune away from the sea, and the beach was having a difficult time holding on to itself against the beating waves and rain. The four friends sat, exposed to the rain, on four saturated lawn chairs. The cold water puddled at their feet and pelted their backs.

John proclaimed, "This storm shall bring the cold water in. We shall not be able to go swimming anymore. My friends, I am sorry to report it. This storm marks the end of our happy summer."

"No swimming!" Margie said, horrified.

"No swimming," said John. "Yes! Sadly, this tempest brings our sweet summer to a close."

Margie seemed devastated. It appeared to be the first time that she had ever considered the concept of seasonal change.

"No more swimming?" she said again. She was shocked, really. "Can it be true?"

"September is the cruelest month," John said.

There was a bag of potato chips open on John's lap, and the rain had made it into a soggy, salty feed bag. He fished some of the damp potato chips out and tossed them over the edge of the house.

"What a storm," observed Peg. "Gosh."

J.J. said reassuringly, "This is nothing, Peg. This isn't even the real storm. The real storm is too busy tearing the shit out of some other place to worry about us."

"J.J. is correct," John announced. "Why, this is just the afterthought of a real storm."

"My goodness," said Margie. "It is raining very hard nonetheless." Then she said, "Peg, sweetheart?"

"Yes," said Peg.

"Is it terribly difficult to get a job if one has a police record?"

"We don't have a police record, Margie."

"Do we not? Did we not just get arrested, this very night?"

"Yeah, but a police record is different. A police record is something you have if you're a career criminal. You can't get a police record until you've committed a string of crimes."

"Peg sounds very confident about this," Margie said.

"For someone who has no idea what the devil she's talking about," said John, "Peg sounds like a veritable attorney general."

"I happen to believe that it is impossible to get a job with a police record," Margie said. "I shall never be able to get another job, and neither shall Peg. We are doomed! John, sweetheart? Will you always take care of me?"

"Naturally," said John.

"But what shall become of Peg? She will have to become a plaything of a rich old man. John, love? Do you know any rich old men who need young playthings?"

John replied, "Only my father. And I imagine that he already has a plaything."

There was an impressive flash of lightning.

"Oh, baby," said J.J.

John stood up. He took his ponytail over one shoulder and wrung it out. He announced, "I have a demand. We shall go swimming. This is our last chance. Let us not hesitate, for tomorrow the water shall be too cold."

"That's funny," J.J. said. "I'm not going swimming."

"That's funny," Peg said. "I'm damn sure not going swimming, either."

"You are both exquisitely funny," John said, "because we actually are going swimming indeed. I demand it."

"Nobody's going swimming tonight, buster," said Peg.

John thrust his fist in the air and shouted, "To the sea! We shall go to the sea with zeal! I demand zeal."

Margie said, "My sweet John has taken leave of his senses."

"The storm will be gone by tomorrow, my friends," John said. "The sun will come out, but the water will already be cold. And you shall be very sorry indeed that you missed your last chance to swim."

"John's senses have simply left him," Margie said.

"This is not even the real storm," John said. "Is that not exactly what J.J. said? No? And J.J. is a sensible man. This is merely the afterthought of a storm. I would be embarrassed to call this a storm."

"I'll go swimming," J.J. said. "What the hell."

Margie looked from Peg to John and then to J.J., who was, in fact, known among the friends as a sensible man. J.J. was slouching with his beer on his stomach. His handsome body was slunk down, low and wet, in the chair, in a terrible posture, like someone's drunken uncle.

"Sure. I'll go swimming," J.J. said. And he added, as an explanation, "We couldn't get much wetter, could we?"

"You got it," said Peg. "That makes sense, I guess."

At that point, it was as though an official decision had been made. It was as if the four friends were a conference of businessmen in strong agreement. It was as if the four friends were four CEOs in consensus, the way they stood up and headed down the stairs, over the dune, and to the beach. When they passed through the front porch, Margie picked up her Dumbo inflatable inner tube and slipped it over her head and around her waist. It was a child's toy, but it amused her. She had taken it swimming all summer. She held Dumbo's plastic gray trunk in her hand, as though it were a divining rod, and followed the head straight ahead to water.

Down at the beach, the spoiled, foolish John and the handsome J.J. took off their shoes and headed into the water, fully dressed. They pushed their way through the rough surf, which was sometimes waist high, sometimes chest high. They pulled their legs up and over and through the water, struggling as though passing through dense, fast-moving mud. John got knocked over immediately by the first wave, but J.J. dived right into it and came out on top of another. John surfaced and cheered and was knocked over again.

Margie stripped to her underwear, but Peg took off only her skirt. Margie ran in after John and J.J., holding the Dumbo tube around her waist and screaming.

Peg stood in the surf for some time and let the tide bury her feet. Two waves was all it took to sink her over her ankles. There was enough dark and rain that she could not see very far past the three heads of her friends out there. She pulled her feet out of the sand and made her way to the surf, right into the face of a wave that stood for a moment above her as high as a chain link fence. The wave fell, and she relaxed and let it roll her. When Peg came up, she was on top of another wave. She saw John and J.J. and Margie in a valley below her, their mouths open. The trunk of Margie's Dumbo tube stuck out of the water like a periscope. A bigger wave came down on Peg, and on her friends, too.

When Peg surfaced again, she could not see her friends. She treaded water and ducked under three waves before she got high enough on a swell to see that they had gone farther out into the ocean. Her boyfriend and her two friends were out to where the waves were rising but not breaking. J.J. was separated from John and Margie, and he was floating on his back. Margie saw Peg and beckoned to her. In ten minutes of swimming, Peg made it over to them. John had lost his ponytail holder, and his hair was floating all around him, like seaweed.

"Isn't it loud?" Margie shouted. "No?"

Peg was out of breath, so she nodded. A long strand of Margie's hair was stuck from the corner of her mouth to her ear, making a black slash across her face, like a wound from a knife fight. They were all treading water gracelessly, spitting seawater and stretching their necks to stay above the rough surface. Except for J.J., who was never graceless. J.J. swam around easily, his stroke as even and strong as though he were doing casual laps in a YMCA, instead of struggling with a storming ocean.

"How deep do you suppose it is, sir?" John shouted.

J.J. laughed, riding on a swell.

"Twenty feet!" J.J. shouted. Then the swell dipped, and he shouted, "No! I take it back. It's ten feet!" A new swell rose, and J.J. said, "No! It's eighteen feet!"

Peg held her nose and went under, pushing herself down and seeking bottom. When she did touch, her foot first hit stones, then something soft. She panicked and kicked until she was at the surface. She tried to wipe the seawater from her eyes, but the rain pushed it back again.

"This would be easier if we were a species that didn't have to breathe," Margie said. Margie, with her Dumbo inner tube supporting her slightly, was less tired than her friends. She was the most cheerful, the least out of breath.

"John, honey?" Margie asked. "How long can *you* go without breathing?"

"Last time it was three hours," John shouted back.

"Goodness!" Margie said.

John laughed and got a mouthful of water, which gagged him. He coughed wetly. Peg looked around and saw that they had been pulled out far past the jetties, a great distance down from the house. Without saying that they were doing so, the four friends began swimming toward the beach. They were trying in a casual way to head home. They were all getting tired, but nobody wanted to speak about it. For some time, they tried to swim toward shore but did not seem to make any progress. They stopped joking with each other and then even stopped speaking.

After a long while, J.J. said, "Oh, fuck."

"What?" Peg asked her boyfriend; she was breathless. "What is it?"

"Jellyfish."

Another considerable silence. By this point they had stopped pretending that they weren't aiming for shore.

Then John shouted out, "J.J.! My friend!"

"Yeah," said J.J.

"I'm getting . . . um . . . rather tired."

"Okay," said J.J. "We'll go in, then."

John rolled his eyes, almost with annoyance. "My legs are killing me," he said.

"We'll go in now," J.J. said. "I'll help you."

"My legs are very . . . um . . . heavy," said John.

"You've got to take off your jeans, John," said J.J. "Can you do that?"

The rain was cold right through the scalps of the friends, and their breathing was wet and sloppy.

John grimaced, trying to get his jeans off. He was going under, coming back up, going under again. J.J. swam behind him and held him up by sticking his arms under John's armpits. John squirmed around more, and then his jeans popped up to the surface, where they floated for a moment, dark, like the hide of a shark, and then sank.

"We're going in," J.J. shouted. "If you girls can make it in, then go. If you can't make it in, don't get tired. Just stay out here."

Peg and Margie did not have the breath to answer.

The boys swam away, and a wave immediately separated them from their girlfriends. The girls watched them for a while. It looked as though the boys couldn't make it past the jetties.

Margie's teeth chattered. Peg swam over to her and grabbed Dumbo's inflatable head.

"No," Margie said. "Mine."

"I have to," Peg said. Her legs ached from the cold water. When she kicked hard to warm them, she kicked Margie. Margie started crying. Margie and Peg were pulled up on a wave, and they could see then that John and J.J. were not much closer to the beach. Peg held her breath and shut her eyes. A wave slapped her. She opened her eyes into water and breathed water and swallowed it.

"We won't make it back," Margie said.

Peg kicked her.

"Shut up!" Margie shouted, although Peg had not spoken.

Peg kicked Margie again. The girls treaded water and tried to see the progress of John and J.J. toward the beach. Which, after a great passage of time, the boys did reach. John and J.J. did eventually reach the beach, and when Peg saw this, she said to Margie, "Look!"

"Shut up!" Margie said, and kicked Peg.

Peg could see J.J. pulling John out of the water. J.J. was in fact dragging John from the sea by his hair. A caveman and his wife. J.J. lugged John up the beach and dropped down beside him.

Margie did not look. Her eyes were closed and her mouth was open. Then Peg did not look anymore, either. She could imagine J.J. slouched over John, who may or may not have been breathing. She could imagine J.J. taking some time to throw up the seawater from his gut, lean his forehead against the sand, retch a little.

Then J.J. would stand on his strong and handsome legs, a little shaky. Peg could imagine it. J.J. would look out at the water to where Margie and Peg should be. He would probably not be able to spot them. His ragged breathing would continue, and he would stand, hands on his hips, slightly hunched over. He would look very much like an exhausted and heroic star soccer player, after a remarkable save.

J.J. would stand there. He would have to decide whether to come out after Margie and Peg or telephone the coast guard and wait for help. It didn't matter what he decided, because he would hate Margie and Peg either way. Whatever he decided, he would certainly hate them for it. Peg was sure of that, as she was treading water with her eyes closed. Peg did not have to watch more of this scene unfolding. No, she did not. Peg did not have to see it happen to know what would happen.

J.J. would hate Peg and Margie for demanding that difficult decision from him, just as Peg now hated Margie for crying in the water beside her. Just as Peg now hated spoiled and foolish John for taking his friends out there in the rough ocean. Just as (most of all) Peg now hated her handsome boyfriend J.J. Peg hated J.J. for standing on the beach while she herself got dragged out deeper to sea. She hated him for being a strong swimmer. She hated him for wondering what to decide and for catching his breath, and she hated him (most of all) for hating her.

The Many Things That
Denny Brown Did Not Know
(Age Fifteen)

◆ ◆ ◆

N O FAULT of his own, but Denny Brown did not know very much about his parents and their work. Denny's parents were both nurses. His mother was a nurse in the burn unit at Monroe Memorial Hospital, and his father was a private duty nurse, also known as a visiting nurse. Denny was aware of these facts, naturally, but he did not know much past that.

Denny Brown did not know the extent of horrors that his mother encountered daily in her work at the burn unit. He did not know, for instance, that his mother sometimes cared for patients whose skin was essentially gone. He did not know that his mother was considered an exceptional nurse, who was famous for never losing her stomach and for keeping the other nurses from losing theirs. He did not know that his mother spoke to every burned patient, even the doomed ones, in cool and reassuring tones of conversation, never hinting at the agony of their prospects.

Denny Brown knew even less about his father's nursing career, other than that it was unusual and embarrassing to have a *father* who was a nurse. Mr. Brown sensed his son's shame, which was but one of the many reasons he did not talk about any aspect of his work in the home. There was no way, therefore, that Denny could have known that his father secretly would have preferred to have been a psychiatric nurse rather than a private duty nurse. Back in nursing school, Mr. Brown had trained at a large mental hospital, in the men's ward. He had loved it there, and his patients had adored him. If he'd not actually felt that he could cure his patients, he'd certainly believed himself capable of bettering their lives.

However, there was no mental hospital in Monroe County. Therefore, Denny Brown's father had spent his married life working as a private duty nurse instead of the psychiatric nurse he ought to have been. He worked purely out of economic necessity and did not enjoy his assignments. His talents were unrecognized. His patients were old, dying people. They did not even notice him, except in spare moments, when they came out of their death marches only long enough to be suspicious of him. The patients' families were suspicious as well, always accusing private duty nurses of stealing. Society as a whole, in fact, was suspicious of male nurses. So Mr. Brown was met with skepticism in every new job, in every new home, as though he were something perverse.

What's more, Denny Brown's father believed that private duty nursing was not nursing at all, but merely tending. It frustrated him that he did more bathing and wiping than he did nursing. Year after year, Denny Brown's father sat in home after home, watching over the slow and expensive deaths of one wealthy, aged cancer patient after another.

Denny Brown did not know anything about any of this.

Denny Brown (at age fifteen) did not know that his mother regretted the rough things that she often said. She'd had a wise mouth as a little girl, and she had a wise mouth as a grown woman. She also had a dirty mouth. The wise mouth had always been with her. The dirty mouth came from her year of nursing in Korea during the war. In any case, she often said things that she didn't mean or later was privately sorry for. Very privately sorry.

For instance, there was a young nurse named Beth in the burn unit where Denny's mother worked. Beth had a drinking problem. One day, Beth confessed to Denny's mother that she was pregnant. Beth didn't want to have an abortion but couldn't imagine keeping a child on her own.

Beth said desperately, "I was thinking of selling my baby to a nice, childless couple."

And Denny Brown's mother said, "The way you drink, you could sell that baby to the fucking circus."

Mrs. Brown was instantly mortified at herself. She avoided Beth for days, secretly asking herself, as she often did, *Why am I such a horrible human being?*

At the end of Denny Brown's sophomore year, he was invited to the Monroe High School Academic Awards Banquet. Denny's father had to work, but Mrs. Brown attended. Denny got a handful of awards that night. He was a very good, though not exceptional, student. He was a smart kid, but he did not excel in any particular subject, as he did not know yet whether he was very good at any particular thing. So Denny received a small handful of awards, including a certificate of merit, honoring his participation in something called Youth Art Month.

"Youth Art Month," his mother said on the ride home. "Youth Art Month."

She pronounced it slowly: "Youth . . . Art . . . Month . . ."

She pronounced it quickly: "YouthArtMonth."

She laughed and said, "There's just no right way to say that, is there? That's just an ugly goddamn phrase, isn't it?"

And then Denny Brown's mother recognized her son's silence. And she too was silent for the rest of the drive.

She drove on. She did not speak, but she was thinking of Denny. She was thinking, *He does not know how sorry I am.*

Denny Brown did not know, at the beginning of his sixteenth summer, what he was going to do for a job. He did not know what he was interested in. He did not know what was out there for work.

After a few weeks of looking, he ended up taking a part-time job at the Monroe Country Club. He worked in the men's locker room. It was a fancy, carpeted locker room, fragrant with hidden deodorizing agents. The distinguished men of Monroe Township would use the locker room to dress for the golf course. They would put on their cleated golf shoes, leaving their dress shoes on the floor in front of their lockers. Denny Brown did not know anything about golf, but this was not required for his work. It was Denny's job to polish the men's dress shoes while the men themselves golfed. He shared this job with a sixteen-year-old boy from his neighborhood named Abraham Ryan. There was no apparent reason that two people were needed for the job. Denny did not know why these men needed their shoes polished every day, in the first place. Denny did not know why he had been hired.

Some days, Denny and Abraham would have to polish no more than three pairs of shoes during the entire course of their shift. They took turns. When they weren't working, they were instructed to stay in the corner of the locker room, next to the electric shoe-polishing machine. There was only one stool in the locker room, and Denny and Abraham took turns sitting on it. While one sat, the other would lean against the wall.

Denny and Abraham were supervised by the Monroe Country Club sports and recreation manager, a serious older man named Mr. Deering. Mr. Deering would look in on them every hour or so, and say, "Look sharp, boys. The best men in Monroe come through this door."

There was one more component to their job besides polishing shoes. Denny Brown and Abraham Ryan were also in charge of emptying a small tin ashtray that was kept on a wooden table in one corner of the locker room. Nobody ever sat at this table. Denny did not know why the table was there at all, other than to hold the tin ashtray. An average of four cigarette butts a day collected in that ashtray. Still, since the table was just out of their line of vision, Denny and Abraham sometimes forgot to empty it. Mr. Deering would look in on them and scold them.

"Look sharp now," Mr. Deering would say. "It's your job to keep this place looking sharp, boys."

When Denny described his work at the Monroe Country Club to his mother, she shook her head. She said, "That is *exactly* the kind of job that people in communist countries have."

Then she laughed. Denny laughed, too.

Although he did not really know what she meant.

Denny Brown (at age fifteen) did not know how he had suddenly come to be Russell Kalesky's best friend. He did not know how he had suddenly come to be Paulette Kalesky's boyfriend. Both events had occurred within a month of graduation from tenth grade.

Russell Kalesky and Paulette Kalesky were brother and sister, and they were neighbors of Denny's. As a little kid, Denny Brown had been bullied senseless by Russell Kalesky. Russell was a year older than Denny. Not a big child, but a mean one. These were some of Russell's favorite games — playing with fire in Denny's house, throwing eggs at Denny, treating Denny's pets roughly, and stealing Denny's toys to tuck behind the wheels of parked cars. Also, Russell Kalesky passionately enjoyed punching Denny in the stomach.

However, during Denny Brown's sixteenth summer, he suddenly became Russell Kalesky's best friend. He did not know how this had happened. He knew *when* it happened, though. It happened the day after Russell Kalesky bought himself a car, which cost $150. The car was a huge black eight-cylinder Ford sedan, which actually did not run at all. The previous owner of the Ford — an amateur stock car mechanic — happily towed the car over to the Kaleskys' driveway and dropped it there for Russell "to work on." Denny Brown happened to be walking past the Kalesky house on the morning when Russell began working on the Ford, and Russell said, "Hey, man. Check it out."

Russell had the hood up and was polishing the engine with a rag. Denny Brown came over nervously, but trying not to look nervous. He watched for a while. Russell finally said, "There's another rag, man. You want to help?"

So Denny Brown took up a rag and started polishing Russell Kalesky's car engine. It was an enormous engine. Big enough for two polishers.

"Excellent, right?" Russell Kalesky said.

"Excellent," Denny Brown agreed.

After that, Russell started coming around to the Browns' place every morning, asking for Denny.

"Hey, man," he'd say, "want to work on the car today?"

"Excellent," Denny would say.

Denny Brown did not know a single thing about cars. To be honest, neither did Russell. Together, they would unscrew parts and peer at them. They would crawl underneath the car and tap on things with wrenches. They could pass hours this way. Denny would try to start the engine while Russell leaned over the hood, head cocked, listening. Listening hard. They never had the first idea what they were looking at or listening for.

During rest breaks, they would sit in the front seat of the Ford with the doors open, one foot inside and one foot flat on the driveway. Heads back, eyes half shut. The only part of the Ford that actually worked was the radio, and Russell would find a station and turn it up. They would relax. The other guys in the neighborhood would come around, riding their bikes up to the Kaleskys' house and dropping their bikes into the Kaleskys' yard. Then the neighborhood guys would lean against Russell Kalesky's Ford, arms folded, listening to the radio. Just hanging out.

Occasionally, Russell would say, "Excellent, right?"

"Excellent," the guys would all agree.

They would listen to the radio like that until Russell said, "That's it. Back to work."

Then all the guys in the neighborhood would have to get on their bikes and ride away.

"Stick around, Dennis," Russell would say.

Denny Brown did not know how he had suddenly come to be Russell Kalesky's best friend. He did not know how common it is, in fact, for bullies to eventually befriend their victims. He was not yet completely sure that he would never be punched in the stomach again. Denny simply had no idea how happy it made Russell to have him come over in the mornings and work on the Ford. Denny did not know that this was the happiest thing in Russell's life.

Denny Brown also did not know that Russell Kalesky's older brother, Peter Kalesky, made fun of Russell's car every single time he came home for dinner. Peter Kalesky owned a handsome Chevrolet truck. Peter was twenty years old and lived in his own apartment on the other side of Monroe. Unfortunately, Peter came home for dinner often. Denny Brown did not know anything about Peter's attacks on Russell.

"You know what Ford stands for?" Peter would say. "It stands for 'Fix or Repair Daily.'"

"You know what Ford stands for?" Peter would say. "It stands for 'Found on Road Dead.'"

"You know what Ford stands for?" Peter would say. "It stands for 'Found Out Russell's Dumb.'

"You know why they have rear-window defrost features in Fords?" Peter would say. "To keep your hands warm while you're pushing your car up a fucking hill."

Russell Kalesky put himself to sleep every night with dreams of running his brother Peter over with his shiny Ford. Nobody knew about this. It was Russell's secret comfort. He would dream of driving over Peter, dropping the transmission into reverse, and driving over Peter again. Back and forth, back and forth, back and forth. In his dreams, the car made a gentle *thud* every time it ran over Peter's body. And it was that sweet *thud thud thud* sound that would finally send Russell off to sleep.

In the morning, Russell Kalesky would wake up and go over to Denny Brown's house.

"Want to work on the car, man?" he'd ask.

"Excellent," Denny Brown would say. (Still not knowing — never knowing — why he had been asked.)

As for Paulette Kalesky, she was Russell's older sister. She was eighteen years old. She was the best baby sitter in Monroe County, and she worked constantly, tending to the children of a dozen different families in the neighborhood. Paulette was short, brunette, with large breasts and a careful, neat mouth. She had lovely skin. She walked up and down the streets of the neighborhood, pushing other people's children in carriages, with more children following her on tricycles. She gave piggy-back rides and supervised ice cream cones. She carried Band-Aids and Kleenex in her purse, just like a real mother. The Kaleskys were not the best family in Monroe County, but people liked and trusted Paulette. She was very much in demand as a baby sitter.

At the end of June, Denny Brown was invited over to the Kaleskys' house for dinner. It was Russell Kalesky's birthday.

Mrs. Kalesky made spaghetti. Everybody was there. Peter Ka-
lesky had driven over from his apartment across town, and
Paulette Kalesky had taken a rare night off from baby-sitting.
Denny Brown was the only nonfamily member at the party.
He was seated across the table from Russell, wedged between
Paulette Kalesky and Mr. Kalesky. Russell started to open his
birthday gifts and Paulette just went ahead and put her hand on
Denny's leg, hidden under the table. Denny and Paulette had
only spoken to each other once before this incident. The hand
on the leg made no sense. Nevertheless, Denny Brown (age
fifteen) slid his hand under the table and put it on top of the
hand of Paulette Kalesky (age eighteen). He squeezed her hand.
He did not know where he had learned to do *that*.

Over the course of that summer, Paulette Kalesky and Denny
Brown developed a system. She would let him know where she
was baby-sitting that night, and he would ride his bicycle over
and visit her after eight o'clock, once she had efficiently put the
children to bed. Alone together, Denny Brown and Paulette
Kalesky had hot, hot sex. Incredible sex. He did not know how
or why this system had been established, but there it was. They
were terrifically secretive. Nobody knew anything about Denny
and Paulette. But there it was. Hot sex. Out of nowhere.

At age fifteen, there was so much that Denny Brown did not
know about Paulette Kalesky. She had great big breasts. He
knew that, but he only knew it by discreet observation. Hot sex
notwithstanding, Paulette would never let him see or touch her
chest. She kept her shirt on all the time. Denny did not know
why. The fact was, Paulette had gotten her breasts in fifth grade.
Way too early, way too big. Her brothers, Peter and Russell, had
obviously made huge fun of her about it, as did her schoolmates.
There was a period during sixth grade when she was getting so
regularly mocked that she would cry every morning and beg her
parents not to make her go to school.

Paulette's father had told her, "Big breasts are nice, and some-day you will be happy to have them. In the meantime, you'll just have to be ridiculed."

Paulette continued to get ridiculed throughout high school, with a new twist: some girls in her class were now jealous of her. There was one group, in particular, who called her Paulette the Toilet or Paulette the Slut. But it was not that she was taking anybody's boyfriends. Not by any measure. Denny Brown was her first boyfriend, her first kiss. By that time, she was already finished with high school.

Denny did not know why Paulette Kalesky suddenly liked him any more than he knew why Russell Kalesky suddenly liked him. He had no idea what this was all about.

There was, in truth, a very good explanation for Paulette's attraction to Denny, but it was a secret. Denny Brown would never know about it. Denny Brown would never know that Paulette Kalesky had been a baby sitter for several months in a home where Denny's own father was a visiting nurse. It was in the home of an affluent local family named Hart. Mrs. Hart had a new baby in the very same year that Mr. Hart's father was dying of cancer. In the same house, therefore, the Harts had to tend to a colicky baby girl and an eighty-year-old senile man with a rotting liver. Paulette Kalesky was hired to care for the baby. Mr. Brown was hired to care for the old man. Paulette and Mr. Brown did not spend a lot of personal time together during these months, but their paths did cross in the Harts' house, usually in the kitchen, where Paulette would be making up a bottle while Mr. Brown would be puréeing carrots.

"Do you want a cup of tea?" Mr. Brown would ask Paulette. "Maybe a glass of water? You look tired."

"No, thank you," Paulette would say, who was shy of an adult treating her as if she herself were an adult.

"You're doing a very good job," Mr. Brown once told Paulette. "Mrs. Hart would be lost without you."

Paulette thought that Mr. Brown did a good job, too, the way he nursed old Mr. Hart. She'd seen how he'd brightened and cleaned the sickroom since taking over the role of the primary visiting nurse. Mr. Brown had brought a large, cheerful calendar into the sickroom, which he hung right across from Mr. Hart's bed. He'd also brought in a clock with bright hands, which he propped where the patient could see it. He spoke to old Mr. Hart in the most clear and specific ways, using direct references to time and location. He gave out every possible piece of information, always trying to keep the vanishing Mr. Hart alerted to the world.

"My name is Fred Brown," Mr. Brown would say, at the beginning of every shift. "I am the nurse who takes care of you. I'm going to be here with you for eight hours. Your oldest son, Anthony, hired me. You are staying in Anthony's house."

Throughout the day, Mr. Brown would explain his every move this clearly. And at the end of a typical day, he would say, "Good night, Mr. Hart. It is seven in the evening, and time for me to go home. I will come by to help you again on Wednesday, October fourteenth, at eleven in the morning."

Paulette Kalesky thought that Mr. Brown was a wonderful person and a wonderful nurse. She thought he was the nicest man she had ever met, and she secretly fell in love with him. Eventually old Mr. Hart died of liver cancer, of course. Mr. Brown moved on to another case, so Paulette Kalesky did not see him anymore, except in brief glimpses around the neighborhood. But then, suddenly, Denny Brown started hanging around her house, working on her little brother Russell's Ford.

"Your dad is Fred Brown, isn't he?" Paulette asked Denny, way back in June. It was the first time they had ever spoken. In fact, it would be the only time they spoke before the night that Paulette put her hand on Denny's leg. Denny would never know why she had asked this particular question.

"Sure," said Denny. "He's my dad."

Paulette did not think that Denny looked like his father at all. Nonetheless, she very much hoped that he might grow up to be like his father. Somehow, in some manner. So she secretly fell in love with Denny Brown, for that reason. With that hope.

Naturally, Denny Brown did not know anything about any of this.

As an adult, Denny Brown would look back on his sixteenth summer and think that it was a wonder he was even allowed to leave the house. He would realize how woefully uninformed he was, how woefully unprepared. There was so much information that Denny Brown was missing at age fifteen. Any of it would have helped him. No matter how minor. Later in life, Denny would believe that he had been sent out there knowing nothing. Nobody ever told him anything about anything. He did not know what people did with their lives or what they wanted or regretted. He did not know why people got married or chose jobs or chose friends or hid their breasts. He did not know whether he was good at anything or how to find out. Everybody just let him walk around without knowing a thing.

His education was so incomplete. Denny Brown (at age fifteen) did not know the meaning of any of these words: *ethereal, prosaic, fluvial, paucity, gregarious, vitriol, umbrage, nihilism,* or *coup d'état.* These were among a list of words that he (and every other high school junior in the region) would be taught by the end of the following school year. But he would have to go through his sixteenth summer without having the use of any of those words.

Denny Brown did not know about Euclid or mitosis or Beethoven's deafness, either, but the Monroe County Board of Education was all geared up to teach him those things as well, come September.

And another thing Denny Brown knew nothing about was the very name of his town. What did "Monroe" even mean? He had somehow been allowed to pass through ten grades of Monroe County public schools without ever having learned that his town was named after an American president, James Monroe. Denny Brown thought that "Monroe" was just a word. Denny did not know, therefore, what "Monroe" was referring to, when used in the very central contexts of his life, like Monroe Memorial Hospital or Monroe High School or Monroe Country Club. Denny Brown did not know that James Monroe was a wounded Revolutionary War veteran and a two-term president. Denny certainly did not know that, during his 1820 re-election bid, James Monroe had received every single vote in the electoral college except one — that of a New Hampshire delegate named William Plumber. William Plumber had withheld his vote intentionally, taking it on himself to ensure that no man would ever share with George Washington the honor of a unanimous election to the United States presidency. William Plumber (who was notable in his life for nothing else) believed that stripping George Washington of that singular achievement would have been a national shame, remembered and regretted by every citizen throughout American history.

And yet Denny Brown (at age fifteen) did not even know that the word "Monroe" was a person's name.

Denny Brown knew nothing about where he lived. He did not know that his water came from a reservoir twenty-five miles north of Monroe, or that his electricity came from one of the state's first nuclear plants. He'd spent his life in a suburban housing development called Greenwood Fields, never knowing that the area had once been a dairy farm. He did not know that the land had once belonged to a family of Swedish immigrants named Martinsson, whose only son died in 1917, killed in the trenches of France. Actually, Denny Brown did not yet know what *trenches* were. That was eleventh-grade history. He did not yet know very much about World War I. He knew nothing (and would never really learn) about more obscure wars, like the

Spanish-American War and the Korean War. He did not know that his mother had served for a year as a nurse in the Korean War. She'd never mentioned it.

Denny Brown did not know that his parents had fallen in love literally at first sight, or that his mother was pregnant on her wedding day. He did not know that his Grandmother Brown had objected strongly to the marriage because Denny's mother was older than his father and had a wise mouth. Grandmother Brown thought that Denny's mother was a "whore," and said as much to her son. (That would be *her* only use of dirty language in ninety years on earth, and Denny's father wept at the word.)

Denny Brown did not know that his mother had wept only once in her married life. He could not imagine her ever crying. It was over Denny himself, actually. It happened when Denny was two years old. He had reached up to the stove and pulled a frying pan full of simmering gravy down on top of him. His mother was right there. She grabbed him and threw him into the bathtub, where she ran cold water over him. She tore off his clothing. His mother (the burn unit nurse, the war hospital nurse) became hysterical, screaming for her husband. The baby screamed; the mother screamed. She would not let Denny out from under the stream of cold water, even when he was shivering and his lips were turning blue.

"He's burned!" she screamed. "He's burned! He's burned!"

In fact, Denny turned out to be fine. Mrs. Brown had acted quickly enough, and Denny had received only first-degree burns on his face and hands. But his mother cried for a full day. She thought, *I am not worthy to be a mother.*

What's more, up until the day that Denny was burned, his mother had wanted to have a second child, but she did not ever consider this again. Never again. Denny Brown did not know that he had ever been burned or that his mother had ever cried or that his mother had ever wanted another baby. He did not know anything about any of this.

He did know, however, where babies came from. At age fifteen, he did know that. His mother had taught him that, at the proper age and in the proper manner.

But there was so much else that he did not yet know. He was ignorant on so very many subjects. At age fifteen, for instance, Denny Brown still happened to believe that the Twin Towers were located in the Twin Cities.

On the morning of August 17, during Denny Brown's sixteenth summer, Russell Kalesky came over to the Browns' house, asking for Denny. As usual. Everything that morning was just as usual.

"Want to work on the car today, man?" Russell asked.

"Excellent," Denny said.

But Russell looked different. His face and arms were covered with ugly red spots.

"Are you okay?" Denny asked.

"Check it out," Russell said. "I got the chicken pox, man."

Denny Brown did not know that anybody except little kids could get the chicken pox.

"Mom!" Denny cried, laughing. "Mom! Help!"

Denny's mother, the nurse, came to the door and looked at Russell. She made him lift up his shirt so that she could examine the spots on his chest. This made Russell Kalesky laugh so hard out of embarrassment that a bubble of snot popped out of his nostril, and that made *Denny* laugh so hard that he had to sit down on the front step. Denny and Russell were both laughing like fools.

"You definitely have the chicken pox, Russell," Denny's mother diagnosed.

For some reason, this made Russell and Denny laugh so hard

that they had to fall into each other's arms and then hold on to their stomachs and stamp their feet.

"Although it doesn't seem to be interfering with morale . . ." Denny's mother observed.

Because he had already had the chicken pox, Denny was allowed to go over to the Kaleskys' house. Russell and Denny worked on the Ford for a while. Their job for the day was to take the mirrors off the sides of the car, soak them in a bucket of soapy water, then polish them and return them to their places. Russell kept stepping out of the driveway and into the garage because he said the sun hurt his chicken pox. Every time Russell mentioned the words *chicken pox*, Denny would start laughing again.

"Who gets the chicken pox, man?" Denny asked. "That's crazy, getting the chicken pox."

"My whole goddamn family got it, man," Russell said. "Nobody ever had it before, and the whole family got it. Even my mom got it, man."

Denny laughed. Then he stopped laughing.

"Even Paulette?" he asked. "Did Paulette get it?"

It was the first time Denny Brown had ever said the name *Paulette* around her brother Russell Kalesky.

"Paulette?" Russell said. "Paulette? Paulette's the one that brought it home, man. Shit! She got it the worst. She got it from one of her stupid kids, man."

"Is she . . . um . . . okay?"

Russell was not hearing or recognizing Denny's tone. Russell was not asking himself why Denny Brown would care about his sister, Paulette.

Russell said, "Paulette's a freak, man. She won't come out of her room, man. She's just up there crying all day. '*Wahhh! It itches! Help me!*'"

Denny stood there in the Kaleskys' driveway. He stood there

in the sun, holding a sideview mirror. Stood there and stood there.

"Hey, man," Russell said.

"Hey, man," Russell said again.

Denny Brown looked up at him.

"Hey, man," Russell said.

"I have to go inside now," Denny said.

Denny set the sideview mirror down on the driveway and went into the Kaleskys' house. Mrs. Kalesky was lying on the couch. The shades were drawn in the living room, and the television was on. Mrs. Kalesky was pink with calomine lotion.

"Are you okay?" Denny asked her.

She was smoking a cigarette, and she looked up at him. She was usually a friendly lady, but she didn't smile. She shook her head, in fact, and looked miserable. Her face was covered with lumps and swellings, worse than Russell's.

"I'll be back, Mrs. Kalesky," Denny said. "I'm just going upstairs. I'm just going upstairs for a minute."

Denny went up the stairs of the Kaleskys' house and down the hall to the room he knew was Paulette's. He knocked on the door.

"It's Denny," he said. "It's me."

He went inside. Paulette was on her bed, lying on top of her sheets and blankets. She saw Denny and started to cry. She was worse than Russell and worse than her mother. She put her hands over her face.

"It itches," she said. "It itches so much."

"Okay," Denny said. "Hold on, okay?"

The thing was, Denny had indeed had the chicken pox before. He wasn't that young when he'd had it, either. Almost eleven years old. His mother had been working a lot during that time, and Denny's father had nursed him. Denny's father had done a very good job nursing him, Denny remembered.

Denny went downstairs and into the Kaleskys' kitchen. Russell was inside now, too.

"What the fuck, man?" Russell asked.

"Russell," Mrs. Kalesky said. "No." She was too weak to protest the dirty mouth further.

"Russell," Denny said, "I just need to get some oatmeal."

Denny started looking through the kitchen cabinets.

"What the *fuck*, man?" Russell demanded. No protest this time from Mrs. Kalesky. She was really sick.

Denny found a large container of oatmeal, and said to Russell, "It's for the itching. Paulette needs it, okay?"

He went back upstairs. Russell followed him, silent. Denny ran some water in the upstairs bathtub of the Kaleskys' house. He poured the full container of oatmeal into the bath and tested the water temperature, rolling one sleeve up and dipping his arm into the tub. He swirled the oatmeal around and left the water running.

Denny went back into Paulette's bedroom. He passed Russell without speaking.

"Paulette," Denny said, "you're going to sit in the bathtub for a little while, okay? That helps. It helps the itching. I'm going to sit with you, okay?"

He helped her sit up in bed, and then he led her into the bathroom. She was still crying, although not as much. He was holding her hand as they passed by the astonished former bully, Russell Kalesky, who was still standing in the hallway.

"Excuse me," Denny said politely to Russell. "Sorry."

Denny took Paulette into the bathroom and shut and locked the door behind them.

"Okay," he said to her. "Here we go, okay?"

Paulette was wearing her pajamas. They were damp with perspiration. She was very, very sick.

"Okay," Denny said. "You're going to have to get undressed, okay?"

Paulette put her hand on the sink, to steady herself. She took off her socks, one at a time. She stepped out of her pajama bottoms. Then she stepped out of her underwear. She stood there.

"Okay," Denny said. "I'm going to help you out of this shirt, and then we're going to put you in the bathtub, okay? You're going to feel a lot better, okay? Okay? Lift up your arms, Paulette."

Paulette stood there.

"Here we go," Denny said. "Lift up your arms."

Paulette lifted her arms up, like a little girl who needs help getting out of a nightgown. Denny pulled her pajama top over her head.

"Okay," Denny said. "Looks like you have the worst of it on your stomach."

"Look at my skin!" Paulette said, and started to cry again.

"Your skin is going to be fine, okay?" Denny said.

He tested the water again, which was lukewarm. Cool and reassuring tones of water temperature. He swirled the oatmeal once more in the bath and helped Paulette step in.

"That feels better, right?" Denny Brown (age fifteen) said. "That helps, doesn't it?"

She sat in the bath, knees up to her chest. She put her head on her knees, still crying.

"Here we go," Denny Brown said. He scooped up handfuls of wet, cool oatmeal and pressed them on her back, against the patches of mean, swollen pox. "Here we go. Here we go."

Denny packed the cool oatmeal against her neck and shoulders and arms. He took a cup from the sink and ran water over her head to calm the itching under her hair. He ran warmer water into the tub when its temperature began to drop.

Denny Brown knelt on the floor beside Paulette. Downstairs on the couch, Mrs. Kalesky wondered what was going on up there. Upstairs in the hallway, the former bully Russell Kalesky sat down on the floor, directly across from the locked bathroom door. Russell stared at the door. He tried to hear what was going on in there, but he could hear nothing.

Inside the bathroom, Denny was tending Paulette. "You can lean back now," he told her.

He helped ease her from the sitting position until she lay back in the bathtub. He put a folded towel under her head as a pillow. The water was cool and high all around her, reaching just below her chin. Her breasts floated up. They were lightened by the water.

"You're going to feel better in exactly five minutes," Denny Brown said, and smiled at her. Then he said, "Do you want a glass of water?"

"No, thank you," Paulette said.

Maybe five minutes passed. Five minutes probably did pass. Mrs. Kalesky waited downstairs, still wondering what was going on. A few houses away, Denny Brown's mother got ready to go to work at the burn unit. Denny Brown's father helped a dying patient across town eat some lunch. Monroe High School sat empty. Russell Kalesky's Ford sat in the driveway, still as ever. It was August. All things were as they always are in August.

And then Paulette Kalesky said to Denny Brown, "You're doing a good job."

Just outside the bathroom, Russell Kalesky sat very still indeed. He did not know what his friend was doing in there. He did not know what his sister was doing in there. Russell did not know what he was watching for, but he watched that bathroom door as closely as any person can watch anything. He did not know what he was listening for, either. But Russell Kalesky listened, and his head was cocked sharply.

The Names of
Flowers and Girls

✦ ✦ ✦

A T THE TIME of Babette, my grandfather was not yet
twenty. Although today, and perhaps even then, such
youth is not necessarily married to innocence, in his case
it was. There were boys his age who had already served in the
war and returned, but he was not among them, for the unro-
mantic reason that one of his feet was several sizes larger than
the other. Outfitting him with boots would have inconven-
ienced the United States Army enough that he was not selected,
and he passed the war years, as before, in the company of his
elderly great-aunt.

On this particular Wednesday night, he chose not to tell his
aunt where he was going. This was not out of deviousness, for
he was not by nature a liar. Rather, he believed that she would
not have understood or even heard him in the advanced stage of
her senility. He did ask the neighbor, a widow with bad knees,
to look in on his aunt throughout the evening, and she agreed
to. He had already been to a boxing match the month before,
and had briefly, late one Saturday, stood in the doorway of a
loud and dangerous local bar, so this was not his first attempt to

observe a seediness he had never known. He learned little out of those first two experiences, however, except that the smell of tobacco smoke clings stubbornly to hair and clothing. He had higher hopes for this evening.

The nightclub he found was considerably darker inside than the street outside had been. It was an early show, a weekday show, but the place had already filled with a shifting, smoking audience of men. The few lights around the orchestra dimmed just as he entered, and he was forced to feel his way to a seat, stepping over feet and knees in the aisle. He tried not to touch people, but brushed nonetheless against wool and skin with every move until he found an empty seat and took it.

"Time?" a voice beside him demanded. My grandfather tensed, but did not answer.

"The time?" the voice questioned again. My grandfather asked quietly, "Are you talking to me?"

There was a sudden spotlight on the stage, and the question was forgotten. Babette began to sing, although at that time, of course, he did not know her name. When his eyes adjusted to the glaring white light, it was only the color of her dress that he saw — a vivid green that today we call lime. It is a color decidedly not found in nature but is now manufactured artificially for the dying of paint, clothing, and food. It cannot shock us anymore; we are too familiar with it. In 1919, however, there were not yet cars to be found in that shade, or small houses in the suburbs, or, one would suspect, fabric.

Nonetheless, Babette wore it, sleeveless and short. My grandfather did not at first even notice that she was singing, on account of that vivid lime-green dress. She was not a gifted singer, but it is almost petty to say so, as musical ability was clearly not required for her job. What she did, and did well, was move in swaying, dancing steps on very pleasant legs. Novelists writing only a decade before that night still referred to beautiful women as having "rounded, well-shaped arms." By the end of

World War I, however, fashion had changed such that other features were now visible, and arms got considerably less attention than they once had. This was unfortunate, for Babette's arms were lovely, perhaps even her best feature. My grandfather, however, was not very modern, even as a young man, and he noticed Babette's arms appreciatively.

The lights at the back of the stage had risen, and there were several dancing couples now behind Babette. They were adequate, efficient dancers — the men slender and dark, the women in short swinging dresses. The nature of the lighting muted the shades of their clothing into uniform browns and grays, and my grandfather could do little more than note their presence and then resume staring at Babette.

He was not familiar enough with show business to know that what he was watching was the insignificant opening act of what would be a long bawdy night of performance. This particular number was no more than an excuse to open the curtain on something other than an empty stage, to warm up the small orchestra, and to alert the audience that the evening was commencing. There was nothing risqué about Babette except the length of her hemline, and it is likely that my grandfather was the only member of the audience who felt any excitement at what he was watching. It is almost certain that none of the other men around him were clutching at their trousers with damp hands or moving their lips, silently searching for words to describe that dress, those arms, that startling red hair and lipstick. Most of the audience had already heard the song on a recording made by a prettier, more talented girl than Babette, but my grandfather knew very little of popular music or of pretty girls.

When the performers bowed and the lights dimmed, he jumped from his seat and moved quickly back over the men in his row, stepping on feet, stumbling, apologizing for his clumsiness in a low murmur. He felt his way up the center aisle and to the heavy doors, which threw quick triangles of light on the floor behind him as he pushed them open. He ran into the lobby and caught an usher by the arm.

"I need to speak with the singer," he said.

The usher, my grandfather's age but a veteran of the war, asked, "Who?"

"The singer. The one with the red, the red — " He pulled at his own hair in frustration.

"The redhead," the usher finished.

"Yes."

"She's with the visiting troupe."

"Yes, good, good," my grandfather said, nodding foolishly. "Wonderful!"

"What do you need with her?"

"I need to speak with her," he repeated.

Perhaps the usher, seeing that my grandfather was sober and young, thought that he was a messenger boy, or perhaps he only wanted to be left alone. In any case, he led him to Babette's room, which was under the stage in a dark, door-lined hall.

"Someone here to see you, miss," he said, knocking twice and leaving before she answered.

Babette opened the door and looked down the hall at the departing usher, and then at my grandfather. She wore a slip and had a large pink towel wrapped around her shoulders like a shawl.

"Yes?" she asked, lifting her high, arched eyebrows even higher.

"I need to speak with you," my grandfather said.

She looked him over. He was tall and pale, in a clean, inexpensive suit, and he carried his folded overcoat under one arm as if it were a football. He had a bad habit of stooping, but now, out of nervousness, was standing perfectly straight. This posture helped his appearance somewhat, forcing his chin out and lending his shoulders a width they did not generally seem to have.

There was nothing about him that would have compelled Babette to shut the door in his face, so she remained there before him in her slip and towel.

"Yes?" she asked again.

"I want to paint you," he said, and she frowned and took a step back. My grandfather thought with alarm that she had misunderstood him to mean that he wanted to apply paint to her body, as one would paint a wall, and, horrified, he explained, "I meant that I would like to paint a picture of you, a portrait of you!"

"Right now?" she asked, and he answered quickly, "No, no, not now. But I would like to, you see. I would love to."

"You're a painter?" she asked.

"Oh, I'm terrible," my grandfather said. "I'm a terrible painter, I'm ghastly."

She laughed at him. "I've already had my picture painted by several artists," she lied.

"Certainly you have," he said.

"You saw me sing?" she asked, and he said that he had indeed.

"You aren't staying for the rest of the show?" she asked, and he paused before answering, realizing only then that there was a show other than what he had seen.

"No," he said. "I didn't want to miss you. I was afraid you might leave right away."

She shrugged. "I don't let men into my dressing room."

"Of course you don't!" he said, hoping he had not insinuated that he expected an invitation. "I had no intention of that."

"But I'm not going to stand in this hallway and talk to you," she continued.

My grandfather said, "I'm sorry that I disturbed you," and unfolded his overcoat to put it on.

"What I mean is that if you want to talk to me, you're just going to have to come inside," Babette explained.

"I couldn't; I didn't mean to —"

But she had already stepped back into the small, poorly lit room and was holding the door open for him. He followed her in, and when she shut the door, he leaned against it, anxious to intrude as little as possible. Babette pulled an old piano stool over to the sink and looked at herself in a silver hand mirror. She ran the water until it was hot, dampened two fingers, and pressed a curl just behind her ear back into shape. Then she looked at my grandfather over her shoulder.

"Now why don't you tell me just what it was that you wanted."

"I wanted to draw you, to paint you."

"But you say you're no good."

"Yes."

"You shouldn't say that," Babette said. "If you're going to be something, if you're going to be someone, you've got to start telling people that you're good."

"I can't," he said. "I'm not."

"Well, it's easy enough to say that you are. Go on, say it. Say, 'I am a good artist.' Go on."

"I can't," he repeated. "I'm not one."

She picked up an eyebrow pencil off the edge of the sink and tossed it to him.

"Draw something," she said.

"Where?"

"Anywhere. On this wall, on that wall, anywhere. Doesn't matter to me."

He hesitated.

"Go on," she said. "It's not as if you could make this room look any worse, if that's what you're worried about."

He found a spot next to the sink where the paint wasn't too badly chipped or marked with graffiti. Slowly, he began to draw a hand holding a fork. Babette stood behind him, leaning forward, watching over his shoulder.

"It's not a good angle for me," he said, but she did not answer, so he continued. He added a man's forearm and wristwatch.

"It's smudging like that because the pencil is so soft," he apologized, and she said, "Stop talking about it. Just finish it."

"It is finished." He stepped back. "It's already finished."

She looked at him, and then at the sketch. "But that's just a hand. There's no person, no face."

"See, I'm no good. I told you I was no good."

"No." Babette said. "I think you're very good. I think this is an excellent hand and fork. From just this I'd let you paint my portrait. It's just that it's a queer thing to draw on a wall, don't you think?"

"I don't know," he said. "I never drew on a wall before."

"Well, it's a nice drawing," Babette decided. "I think you're a good artist."

"Thank you."

"You should tell me that I'm a good singer now."

"But you are!" he said. "You're wonderful."

"Aren't you sweet to say so." Babette smiled graciously. "But I'm really not. There are no good singers in places like this. There are some fine dancers, and I'm not a bad dancer, but I'm a terrible singer."

He didn't know what to say to this, but she was looking at him as if it was his turn to speak, so he asked, "What's your name?"

"Babette," she said. "And when a girl criticizes herself, you really should crawl to the ends of the earth to contradict her, you know."

"I'm sorry," he said. "I didn't know."

She looked at herself in the mirror again. "So do you want to only paint my hand?" she asked. "I haven't got a fork with me."

"No," he said. "I want to paint you, all of you, surrounded by black, surrounded by a whole crowd of black. But there will be a white light, and you in the center" — he lifted his hands to show placement in an imaginary frame — "in the center in green and red." He dropped his hands. "You should've seen that green and that red."

"Well, it's just the dress you like, then," she said. "Just the dress and the hair."

And your arms, he thought, but only nodded.

"None of that is really me, though," Babette said. "Even my hair is fake."

"Fake?"

"Yes. Fake. Dyed. Please don't look so shocked. Really, you can't have ever seen this color hair before."

"No!" my grandfather almost shouted. "I never had. I think that's exciting, that you can make it that way if you like. I wondered about it, but I didn't think, of course, that it had been dyed. I think that there are so many colors I've never seen — could I touch it?"

"No," Babette said. She reached for a comb from the sink and pulled a single red hair from its teeth. She handed it to him. "You can have this one piece. I'm sure that I don't know you well enough to let you drag your hands all over my head."

He carried the strand to the lamp and stretched it taut under the bulb, frowning in concentration.

"It's brown at one end," he said.

"That's the new growth," she explained.

"Your real hair?"

"The whole thing is my real hair. That brown is my real color."

"Just like mine," he said in surprise. "But you'd never know it to see you onstage. I tell you, you'd never imagine we two would have the same sort of hair. Isn't that remarkable?"

Babette shrugged. "I wouldn't say it was remarkable. But I suppose I'm used to my hair."

"Yes, I suppose you are."

"You're not from New York City, are you?" she asked.

"Yes, I am. I've always lived here."

"Well, you don't act like it. You act just like a little boy from the country. Don't be put off by that, now. It's not a bad thing."

"I think it is. I think it's awful. It comes of not talking to enough people."

"What do you do all day, then?"

"I work in the back of a print shop sometimes. And I live with my great-aunt."

"And she's very old," Babette said.

"Yes. And senile. All she can remember anymore are the names of flowers and girls."

"What?"

"The names of flowers and girls. I don't know why, but that's how it's become. If I ask her a question, she thinks and thinks, but then finally she'll say something like, 'Queen Anne's Lace, Daisy, Emily, Iris, Violet . . .'"

"No!" Babette said. "I think *that's* remarkable. She must be very pretty to listen to."

"Sometimes. Sometimes it's just sad, because I can see how frustrated she is. Other times she just lets herself talk and strings them all together: 'Ivy-Buttercup-Catherine-Pearl-Poppy-Lily-Rose.' Then it's pretty to listen to."

"I'm sure that it is," Babette said. "You forget how many flowers' names are girls' names, too."

"Yes." My grandfather nodded. "I've noticed that."

"She used to take care of you, didn't she?"

"Yes," he said. "When I was young."

"You still are young." Babette laughed. "I'm even young, and I think I'm much older than you."

"I couldn't imagine how old you are. I hadn't even thought about it."

"I can see why you wouldn't." Babette lifted her mirror again and looked at herself. "All this makeup covers everything. It's hard to tell what I look like at all. I think I'm pretty, anyway, but I only realized this week that I'm not going to age well. Some women I know look like girls their whole lives, and I suspect that it's on account of their skin. From a distance I still look fine, and onstage I'll look wonderful for years, but if you come close to me, you'll see the change already."

She jumped up and ran in two steps to the opposite corner of the room from my grandfather.

"You see, I'm just heavenly from here," she said, and then leaped right up to him so that their noses almost touched. "But now look at me. See the little lines here and here?" She pointed to the outer corner of each eye. My grandfather saw nothing like lines, only quickly blinking lashes and makeup. He noticed that her breath smelled of cigarettes and oranges, and then he stopped breathing, afraid that he might touch her somehow, or do something wrong. She took a step back, and he exhaled.

"But it's like that with everything you look at too closely," Babette continued. The green dress that she had worn earlier was hanging over a low ceiling pipe. She pulled the dress down and backed into the far corner again, holding it up against herself. "Just look at this lovely green thing," she said. "Onstage it'll turn a man's head, won't it? And I looked so swish in it, didn't you think?"

My grandfather said that he had thought just that. She approached him again, although, to his relief, she did not stand so close this time.

"But you can see what a cheap thing it really is," she said, turning the dress inside out. "It looks just like a child sewed those seams, and it's all kept together with pins. And feel it. Go on."

My grandfather lifted a bit of the skirt in one hand, although he did not really feel the material as he had been told to.

"You can tell right away that it's not really silk, that there isn't actually anything nice about it at all. If I wore this to someone's home, I would look just like some kind of street girl. It's pathetic." She turned from him, and, over her shoulder, she added, "I will spare you the smell of the thing. I'm certain that you can imagine it."

Actually, he couldn't begin to imagine what it smelled like. Cigarettes and oranges, he suspected, but he had no way of knowing. Babette let her pink towel slide to the floor, and then turned and faced my grandfather in only her slip and stockings.

"I would guess that I look very nice this way," she said, "although I don't have a large mirror, so I'm not sure. But if I were to take this slip off, and if you were to come over here next to me, you'd see that I have all sorts of bumps and hairs and freckles, and you might be very disappointed. You've never seen a naked woman, have you?"

"Yes, I have," he said, and Babette looked at him in quick surprise.

"You have never," she said sharply. "You have never in your life."

"I have. It's been three years now that my aunt can't care for herself. I keep her clean, change her clothes, give her baths."

Babette winced. "I think that must be disgusting." She picked up the towel from the floor and wrapped it around her shoulders again. "She probably can't even control herself anymore. She's probably all covered with nasty messes."

"I keep her very clean," he said. "I make sure that she —"

"No." Babette held up her hands. "I can't listen to that, any of that. I'll be sick, really I will."

"I'm sorry," my grandfather said. "I didn't mean —"

"That doesn't disgust you? To do those things?" she interrupted.

"No," he said honestly. "I think it must be just like taking care of a baby, don't you?"

"No. Absolutely not. Isn't that funny, though, that I would be so disgusted by what you just told me? I'm sure there are things in my life that would shock you, but I didn't think that you could shock me."

"I didn't mean to shock you," he apologized. "I was only answering your question."

"Now I'll tell you something shocking," she said. "When I was a little girl in Elmira, we lived next to a very old man, a Civil War veteran. He'd had his arm amputated during a battle, but he wouldn't let the surgeon throw it away. Instead, he kept it, let all the skin rot off, dried it in the sun, and took it home. A souvenir. He kept it until he died. He used to chase his grand-children around the yard with it, and then beat them with his own arm bone. And one time he sat me down and showed me the tiny crack from where he'd broken it when he was a boy. So do you think that's disgusting?"

"No," my grandfather said. "It's interesting. I never met any-one from the Civil War."

"Now that's funny," Babette said, "because everyone I ever told that to was shocked, but it never shocked me. So why can't I listen to you talk about cleaning up your old aunt?"

"I don't know," he said. "Except that your story was a lot more interesting."

"I didn't think I still could be disgusted," she said. "I'll tell you another story. The church in my hometown used to have ice cream socials for the children, and we would eat so much that we would get sick. But it was such a treat that we wanted more, so we used to go outside, vomit what we'd eaten, and run back in for more. Pretty soon all the dogs in town would be at the church, eating up that melting ice cream as fast as we could throw it up. Do you think that's disgusting?"

"No," my grandfather said. "I think that's funny."

"So do I. I did then, and I still do." She was quiet for a moment. "Still, there are things that I've seen in the last few years that would make you sick to hear. I could shock you. I've done things that are so awful, I wouldn't tell you about them if you begged me to."

"I wouldn't do that. I don't want to know," he said, although when he had left his home that evening, he had wanted just that sort of information, desperately.

"It's not important, anyhow. We won't talk about it at all. You're a funny one, though, aren't you? I feel just like an old whore saying that. There are so many old whores in this business, and they all look at young men and say, 'You're a funny one, aren't you?' It's true, though, with you. Most men get a sniff of a girl's past and want to know every single thing she's ever done. And you keep looking at me, but not like I'm used to."

My grandfather blushed. "I'm sorry if I stared," he said.

"But not just at me! You've been staring at the whole room. I'll bet you've memorized every crack on these walls, the rungs on the bed frame, and what I've got in the bottom of my suitcases, too."

"No."

"Yes, you have. And you've been memorizing me. I'm sure of it."

He did not answer her, because, of course, she was absolutely right. Instead, he nervously shifted his weight back and forth, suddenly acutely aware of the different sizes of his feet. Not for the first time in his life, he felt unbalanced from the ground up because of this deformity, almost dizzy from it.

"Now I've made you flustered," Babette said. "I think that's easy enough to do, so I won't be proud." After a pause, she added, "I believe you really are an artist because of how you've been staring. You're a watcher, not a listener. Am I right?"

"I don't know what you mean," he said.

"Hum me a bar from my song tonight, or even tell me a line from the chorus. Go on."

He thought back quickly, and at first could only come up

with the sound of the faceless man beside him demanding the time. Then he said, "You sang something about being blue because someone left, a man, I think . . ." He trailed off, then added weakly, "It was a pretty song. You sang it well."

She laughed. "It's just as well that you didn't listen. It's a stupid song. But tell me, how many couples were dancing behind me?"

"Four," he answered without hesitation.

"And who was the smallest girl onstage?"

"You were."

"And how big was the orchestra?"

"I couldn't see, except the conductor, and the bass player, of course, because he was standing."

"Yes, of course." Babette walked to the sink, and spent a few moments doing something with the toiletries there. Then she turned and approached him with one arm outstretched. She had striped the white underside of her forearm with five short strokes of lipstick, each shade only slightly different from the one beside it. She covered her mouth with her other hand and asked, "Which color do I have on my lips right now?"

My grandfather looked down at her arm, unexpectedly alarmed at the slashes of red across the white skin. He paused before answering, because something else had caught his eye, a faint, bluish vein that ran diagonally across the inside bend of her elbow. Then he pointed to the second lipstick stripe from her wrist and said assuredly, almost absently, "This one."

He looked up at her face only after she had let her arm drop, and the intriguing blue vein vanished from view. She was still holding her other hand to her mouth and staring at him with eyes so wide and spooked that it seemed as if her hand belonged to a stranger, an attacker. He slowly pulled her arm down away from her face and looked at her in silence. He looked at her lips and confirmed that he had chosen correctly. Without thinking about what he was beginning to do, he lifted her chin so that her face was out of shadow and studied the shape of her fore-head, nose, and jaw. Babette watched him.

"Look," she said. "If you're going to kiss me, just —"

She stopped talking as he released her chin and took hold of her wrist, turning it over and exposing where she had marked herself with the lipsticks. He stared for a long while, and she finally began to rub at the smearing red lines with the corner of her towel, as if embarrassed now by what she had done. But my grandfather wasn't looking at that. He was studying that faint blue vein again, examining its short path across its cradle, the soft fold of her arm. After some time, he lifted her other arm and compared the twin vein there, holding her wrists gently, but with a thorough self-absorption that negated the lightness of his touch. She pulled away, and he released his hold without speaking.

He crossed the room and looked once more at the dress, carefully noting the alarming green again, frowning. Then he returned to Babette to confirm the color of her hair. He reached up to touch it, but she caught his arm.

"Please," she said. "That's enough."

My grandfather blinked as if she had just woken him from a nap or delivered a piece of unexpected bad news. He glanced around the room as though searching for someone else, some-one more familiar, and then frowned and looked back at Babette.

"You should know that there are ways to act," she said evenly. "There are things to say so that a girl doesn't have to feel used." Her face was empty of expression, but she had lifted the hand mirror and was holding it tightly, as one might hold a tennis racket or a weapon.

He blushed. "I'm sorry," he stammered. "I didn't mean . . . I get that way sometimes, looking, staring like that —"

Babette cut him off with a sharp, irritated glance that crossed her face as fast and dark as a shadow.

"You can't do that to people," she said. He started to apologize again, but she shook her head. Finally she continued, "It's going to be a very good painting, but not very flattering to me. Which is fine," she added, shrugging cavalierly, "because I'll never see it."

"I'm sorry," he repeated, feeling and sounding like a stranger, as if he was once more standing outside her door in the dark cobwebbed hall beneath the stage.

She shrugged one shoulder and lifted a hand to touch a red curl that was already in place. My grandfather watched, silent.

"Don't you think you should leave now?" Babette asked at last.

He nodded, disgusted by the futility of apology, and left. He found his way through the dark hall and out of the nightclub alone, not needing, or even remembering, the young usher who had led him to Babette. Outside it had stopped raining. His overcoat had dried in her room, and he had already forgotten that it had ever been wet.

The widow with the bad knees was waiting for him when he got home. She did not question where he had been, but said only that his aunt was asleep in her chair and had been quiet all night.

"I gave her some soup," she whispered as he unlocked the door.

"Thank you," he said. "You're very kind."

My grandfather closed the door quietly behind him and took off his shoes so that he wouldn't wake his aunt when he passed through the sitting room. In his own bedroom, he began working on what would be the first important painting of his career. He filled several pages with the charcoal-smudged, faceless crowd of the nightclub audience, leaving an empty white space in each sketch, always in the same spot. After several hours, he examined his work, irritated to see that all the pictures were identical: uniformly solid and dark, with a gaping opening in the center for a singer he didn't know how to begin to draw.

He laid his head down on his sleeve and shut his eyes. He breathed in the tobacco smell of his shirt, at first inadvertently and then with great purpose, as if his skill would be enhanced if he deeply inhaled that dank odor. After some time, he opened his small box of oil paints and began trying to mix the green of Babette's dress.

Although later in his life his mastery of color would be considered unrivaled, that night, as a young man with a limited collection of oils, he was overwhelmed by the task of recalling the shade. He worked carefully and several times felt that he was close to success, but found that, as the paint dried, the effect was lost, the color dulled. He was struck by the inevitability of his own limitations.

His desk was covered already with torn pieces of paper and patches of sticky, inadequate green. He looked at the charcoal sketches again and thought about what Babette had said. She was correct to say that it would be a good painting, but wrong to think that it would not flatter her. My grandfather visualized the figure that he knew would eventually fill the empty white space, and he was certain that it would be a very appealing character. Nonetheless, the painting was destined, in his mind, to remain a clumsy rendition of a transient, fantastic moment. It was he, ultimately, who would not be flattered by this work. It was his misfortune to realize this so young.

He heard a sound and set his sketchbook down on the floor. His aunt was talking, and he wondered how long she had been awake. He went into the sitting room, where he turned on a small reading lamp. She was rocking slowly, and he listened for a while to her mumbling.

"Black-eyed Susan," she said, "Grace, Anna, Marigold, Pansy, Sarah . . ."

She had become smaller with age. In this lighting, however, with dark blankets over her legs and embroidered pillows around her, she appeared stately if not strong. My grandfather sat at her feet like a child waiting for a story.

"Lady's slipper, Rosehip, Faith, Zinnia, Cowbell," she said.

He rested his head on her knee, and she stopped talking. She laid her hand on his head and kept it there, where it trembled with the constant palsy of old age. He began to fall asleep and, in fact, had dozed off when she woke him by saying, "Baby." He half-opened his eyes without lifting his head, not sure what he had heard.

She repeated the word, again and again, in the same low tone as her strange, rambling lists.

"Baby, baby, baby," she said, and in his distracted exhaustion, he misunderstood her. He believed that she was saying "Babette," over and over. Of all the flowers and girls, he thought, it was this rich, painful name that she had finally settled on to repeat and repeat and repeat.

He closed his eyes. Even shut, they ached, as if somehow they had been forced to look on himself in sixty years: elderly and dying, calling to his daughters and his granddaughters, calling them all to him, calling them all Babette.

At the Bronx Terminal
Vegetable Market

◆ ◆ ◆

J IMMY MORAN was still very young — barely over forty —
when he started having serious back pains. His family doctor told him that he probably needed an operation on a disc,
and a second doctor (an expensive specialist) confirmed it. Both
doctors agreed that Jimmy would need to take six months off
from work. He would need to lie on his back and do absolutely
nothing at all for six months, and only then would he have a
chance at complete recovery.

"Six months!" Jimmy told the doctors. "I'm in the produce
business, buddies! Are you kidding me?"

Six months! He made his doctors an offer of four months,
which was still much more time than he could afford to lose.
They finally came down to five months, but only grudgingly
and with obvious disapproval. Even five months off was ridiculous. He'd never taken as much as a week away from the Bronx
Terminal Vegetable Market since he'd started working there as a
loading porter, in the summer of 1970. Five months! He had a
wife to support and so many kids at home that it was almost
embarrassing to say the full number. But there was no getting

around any of this. His back was injured and he needed the surgery, so he went ahead with it. And here's how they survived: his wife, Gina, took extra hours at her job; they emptied their small savings account; his brother Patrick gave them some money. Things were not as bad as they might have been.

As it turned out, Jimmy Moran ended up accomplishing two important things during his time away from the market. First of all, he bought a gorgeous 1956 blue Chrysler sedan, which was in great shape and drove like a luxury ocean liner. Gina didn't agree with the investment, but they needed another car, and the Chrysler was a lot cheaper than anything new. Besides, he bought it off an old man in Pelham Bay who hadn't taken the thing out of the garage for decades and had no idea what it was worth. Honestly, the car was a steal. It really was. Jimmy had always wanted a beautiful old car. He'd always felt that he *deserved* a beautiful old car, because he would appreciate it and take good care of it and when he drove around town he would wear a good-looking, old-fashioned kind of brimmed hat, just like his dad used to wear.

His second accomplishment was that he decided to run for president of his union local.

The current president of the Teamsters Local 418 was a guy named Joseph D. DiCello, who had the obvious advantage of being an incumbent *and* an Italian. Most of the union members at the Bronx Terminal Vegetable Market were Italian, and if even half the Italians voted for DiCello, Jimmy Moran would get whipped like a bad dog, and he realized that completely. Jimmy, however, still believed that he had a chance to win. Reason being, Joseph D. DiCello was basically an idiot and a corrupted, useless fuck.

DiCello drove a big Bonneville and hadn't successfully defended a worker's grievance in six years. He barely even showed up at the Bronx Terminal Vegetable Market at all anymore, and when he did show up, he'd always be sure to bring some prostitute with him, picked up from around the gates outside. A Chinese prostitute, usually. DiCello would ask some tired, overworked porter, "Hey, kid? You like my wife? You like my new wife, kid?"

And the porter, naturally, would say something like "Sure, boss."

Then DiCello would laugh at the poor guy, and even the Chinese prostitute would laugh at the poor guy. Therefore, and for numerous other reasons, people were basically getting sick of Joseph D. DiCello.

Jimmy Moran, on the other hand, was a well-liked person. The few Irish workers left at the market would vote for him out of instinct, and Jimmy got along with most of the Italians just fine. Why, he'd even married an Italian. His own kids were half Italian. He had no problems with Italians. He had no problems with the Portuguese, either, and did not think in any way that they were thieves by nature. He also had no problems with the blacks (unlike that sick bigot DiCello), and he was actually quite popular with the Hispanics. Jimmy had held many different jobs over the years at the market, but he'd recently been hired once again as a loading porter, which meant that he worked mostly with Dominicans and Puerto Ricans. Who were all very decent and fun-loving individuals, as far as Jimmy Moran could see.

When it came to the Mexican vote, this would also be no problem. The older Mexicans would remember that, years and years ago, Jimmy Moran had worked at the typically Mexican job of handling and packaging peppers. (And not those sweet Italian bell peppers, either, but pitiless Spanish peppers — jalapeños, poblanos, cayennes, chilies, Jamaican hots — fierce peppers that only Mexicans usually handled, because if a person didn't know what he was doing, he could really get hurt. When a person got the oil from one of those peppers in his eye, it honestly felt just like getting *punched* in the eye.) Although pepper-handling was easy on the back, it was no job for a white man, and Jimmy had quit doing it years and years ago. But he still got along fine with all the older Mexicans, and with most of the younger ones, too.

As for the Koreans, Jimmy had no experience with them. Neither did anybody else, though, so it really didn't matter. It wasn't like Joseph D. DiCello was best friend to the Koreans or anything. The Koreans were strange people, and you could just forget about the Koreans. The Koreans had their own market within the Bronx Terminal Vegetable Market, and they only sold to each other. They talked to each other in Korean, and besides, they weren't even in the union.

There was another thing that Jimmy Moran had in his favor. He was actually a true union man, and not some phony local gangster's kid like DiCello. He wasn't even from the city. He was born in Virginia, and his people were real coal-mining people and honest-to-Christ workingmen. Back in Virginia, when Jimmy was only ten years old, he'd watched his grandfather overturn a company coal truck and empty a shotgun into the engine block during a workers' strike. His uncle was murdered by company detectives, his other uncle died of black lung, his ancestors organized against U.S. Steel, and Jimmy Moran was a true workingman in a way that an affluent cheat like Joseph D. DiCello, for instance, could never be true in a thousand corrupted lifetimes.

Jimmy Moran gave his potential candidacy one evening's thought. This was four months into his recovery from back surgery. He considered all the advantages and disadvantages of staging a campaign, which would be his first. Gina wouldn't be nuts about the idea, but Jimmy's back didn't hurt anymore, he was the owner of a beautiful 1956 Chrysler, and he felt really, really capable. He couldn't think of any reason that he — with his good labor background, his decent personality, and all the different jobs he'd held at the market over the years — should not be the president of the union.

Yes, he gave his candidacy that one evening's thought, and when he woke up the next morning, he was decided. Convicted, even. It was a great feeling. It was like waking up in love.

And so Jimmy Moran returned to the Bronx Terminal Vegetable Market after only four months of recovery. His plan was to campaign for a few nights, and then come back to work officially. He arrived well after midnight, as the delivery trucks were pulling in to load up. When he came through the entrance gate, he stopped to talk with Bahiz, the Arab woman who checked identification cards. She was a fairly attractive woman, so everybody flirted with her. Also, she was the only woman who worked at the entire market, or at least as far as Jimmy Moran had ever noticed in nearly twenty-five years.

"Bahiz!" he said. "Who let you out of the harem?"

"Oh, Jeez. Jimmy's back," she said. She was chewing gum.

"'Jimmy's back!'" Jimmy repeated. "'Jimmy's *back!*' Hey, don't say anything about Jimmy's *back,* sweetheart. You should say, 'Jimmy Moran has *returned.*' Jesus, I don't want to talk about Jimmy's *back.* You like my new car?"

"Very nice."

"Guess what year it is."

"I don't know."

"Just give it a guess."

"I don't know. Nineteen sixty-eight?"

"Are you kidding me?"

"What is it, 'sixty-six? How should I know?"

"Bahiz! It's a 'fifty-six! It's a 'fifty-six, Bahiz!"

"Oh, yeah?"

"Use your eyeballs for once, Bahiz."

"How should I know? I can barely see it."

"The ladies love it, sweetheart. I'll take you for a drive sometime. You never would've refused me all these years if I was driving a car this nice. Isn't that right, Bahiz?"

"Oh, Jimmy. Just go to hell."

"You got a dirty mouth, Bahiz. Listen. How about some figs?"

Sometimes Bahiz had the greatest figs with her. The dried figs that were widely available at the Bronx Terminal Vegetable Market were mostly mission figs, from California. And after eating Bahiz's figs, Jimmy Moran was certainly never going to eat any dried California mission figs again. Some of the better houses at the market carried imported Spanish figs, which were pretty nice, but they were expensive. Also, Spanish figs were kept packaged in plastic-wrapped crates, so it was almost impossible to steal just a handful for free sampling.

Bahiz, however, sometimes had the most incredible Israeli figs, and she would always give a few to Jimmy. Bahiz's mother shipped the figs to her by air mail all the way from the Middle East, which was very expensive but worth it. It was a well-known fact that, throughout all of the entire history of mankind, Israeli figs have always been considered the most valuable figs in the world. Israeli figs taste like granulated honey. They have skins like thin caramels.

But Bahiz didn't have any figs that night.

"Forget about you, Bahiz," Jimmy Moran said. "You worthless old bat."

"I hope somebody hits your dumb-ass car!" she said, and they both smiled at each other and waved good-bye.

Jimmy parked his car in front of Grafton Brothers, which was his most recent employer, one of the biggest wholesale houses in the market and a good place to start his campaign. Grafton Brothers was a very profitable house, and here was why: Salvi and John Grafton bought overripe produce with no shelf life for the lowest, giveaway prices. Then they hired porters to pick through the produce — most of which was rotten — toss out the rotten stuff, and repack the rest of it. Grafton's could triple its investment on a cheap shipment of vegetables while still underselling the rest of the market. It was practically a hoax.

Salvi and John Grafton might have gotten to be rich men this way, with big horse-racing farms down in Florida, but their wholesale empire still smelled like compost from all the ripe food they threw out, and there were more rats at Grafton's than at any other house in the market. Grafton's produce was garbage.

There were specialty houses at the market that took produce very seriously and sold only beautiful fruits and vegetables. There was a Russian Jew in the north docks who flew endive in every day from a small family farm in the middle of Belgium, and that was the finest endive in the *world*. There was a Filipino who sold blackberries in February for five dollars a pint *wholesale*, and buyers were happy to pay, because the blackberries were fantastic and it was worth it. Grafton's was not such a house.

Jimmy Moran had worked for Grafton's off and on over twenty-five years as a porter, a driver, a vegetable sorter, and in practically every other kind of job. The only thing was, he'd never been able to get any kind of desk job inside the barracks of Grafton's offices. Office jobs at the Bronx Terminal Vegetable Market were always a little harder to come by. There was a lot of competition and a lot of pressure, and it helped, apparently, to be good at math. In any case, Grafton Brothers had hundreds of dock employees, and Jimmy knew nearly all of them.

Jimmy Moran walked along the Grafton Brothers docks, carrying on his back a heavy burlap sack filled with the campaign buttons he'd had made up the day before. The buttons said: DICELLO'S NOT ON OUR SIDE, SO LET'S PUT HIM ON THE OUTSIDE. VOTE FOR JIMMY MORAN, PRESIDENT. They were huge buttons, each approximately the diameter of a grapefruit, with black lettering on a yellow background. He moved around the stacks of crates and the vegetable displays and the tractors, and he gave buttons to everybody and talked to everybody. He tried to speak as personally as possible.

He'd say, "Hey, Sammy! Your wife still cooking you those dinners?"

He'd say, "Hey, Len! You still taking all those naps?"

He'd say, "Hey, Sonny! You still work with that other crazy bastard?"

Passing out buttons, shaking hands, passing out buttons, shaking hands, passing out more buttons. Jimmy Moran felt really good. His back wasn't bothering him at all. He felt rested and capable, and it took him several hours to get through Grafton's.

He saw his old friend Herb talking to a young porter, and he said, "Hey, Herb! Who's that, your new boyfriend?"

He saw a porter, not much older than his own son Danny, smoking marijuana behind a melon display, and he said, "Police! You're under arrest, you dope!"

He saw his old friend Angelo playing cards on the back of a crate with some other guys and he said, "What is this, Angelo, a casino?"

Angelo and the others laughed. Everyone asked after his back and hoped he was feeling better. Jimmy Moran had always been popular at Grafton's, and everyone was happy to see him back. He used to do a funny trick when he was working in the cucumber cooler there. He'd pretend to be a blind man. He would stare off into space and put his arms straight out and stumble around, bumping into everybody. He'd say, "I'm the blind vegetable man . . . Excuse me, sir, could you tell me where the cucumbers are?"

There was only one guy who never laughed at that trick, and that was a quiet and serious Haitian porter named Hector.

Jimmy got to the point where he would do the blind-vegetable-man trick only if Hector was around, trying to get Hector to laugh even once. Jimmy would stumble over Hector's feet and feel up Hector's face, and Hector would just stand there, with his arms crossed, not smiling. Eventually, Jimmy would quit it and say, "What is it with you, Hector? Maybe you're the one that's blind."

"Where's that Haitian guy Hector?" Jimmy asked his old friend Angelo. Jimmy's sack of campaign buttons was already half empty. He felt the campaign was going well.

"Hector?" Angelo said. "Hector's a distributor now."

"Get out of here! Hector's a *distributor?*"

"He's in broccoli."

"I go away for a few months and Hector's suddenly a *distributor?*"

Jimmy headed down the Grafton docks to the huge warehouse coolers of broccoli, and, sure enough, there was Hector, in the distributor's shack. Every individual cooler was as big as a furniture warehouse, so every cooler needed a distributor. The distributor's job was to handle the charts and lists showing how much produce was in each cooler and how much produce was going out with each order. It was a pretty good job. If you were good at math, of course, it was a lot easier. Jimmy Moran had actually been hired as a carrot distributor for a few months once, but his friends the dockworkers were always joking around with him and distracting him from doing the job right, so that job didn't work out for Jimmy, and he ended up having to find a porter's job on the docks again.

Of course, the distributors worked on the docks, too. The only thing was, they got to work in little plywood shacks that looked like ice-fishing houses. The shacks had space heaters to fight the cold, and sometimes even had carpeting on the floor.

Hector was in the shack studying his charts, and there was another guy beside him, eating a hamburger.

"Hector!" Jimmy said. "Look at Señor Hector the distributor!"

Hector shook Jimmy's hand through the window of the distributor's shack. Centerfolds of nude black women hung on the wall behind him. Hector wasn't even wearing a jacket in there, just a thin, cotton button-down shirt. A person could really stay warm in a distributor's shack.

"How are things?" Jimmy asked.

"Not bad."

"Who's your friend?"

"This is Ed. He's from the office."

Ed and Jimmy shook hands.

"So, what are you fellas doing over here?" Jimmy asked. "Putting broccoli in small boxes and labeling it twenty-five pounds? What is this, some kind of hoax?"

Hector did not smile. Neither did Ed.

"Listen, Hector, I'm kidding! Listen, I'm running for president of the local."

Jimmy slid two of his campaign buttons over to Hector. "There's one button for each of you," he said.

Hector read his button aloud with his funny accent: "DICELLO'S NOT ON OUR SIDE, SO LET'S PUT HIM ON THE OUTSIDE. VOTE FOR JIMMY MORAN, PRESIDENT."

"You running against *DiCello?*" said the guy from the office named Ed.

"That's right."

Ed stared at Jimmy Moran for a long, long while. He chewed his hamburger in no particular hurry, swallowed, and said finally, "What are you trying to do?"

"What's that?"

"Seriously. What are you trying to do? Get yourself killed?"

"Oh, come on now."

"What do want? You want to wake up in the trunk of a car? Seriously."

Jimmy Moran looked at Hector and shrugged comically. Hector didn't smile, and Ed kept talking.

"What do you want?" he said. "You want to have your legs cut off?"

"I'm not afraid of Joey DiCello," Jimmy said. "And I sure hope you two old boys aren't afraid of him."

"I sure the fuck am afraid of him," Ed said.

"Joey DiCello has no reason to pick on a good guy like me. What do you think — he'll kill me and leave all my kids with no dad? Forget about it."

Ed slid the campaign button back through the window to Jimmy. "You can keep your button, friend."

"Vote for me, and things will really change around here."

Hector still said nothing, but Ed asked, "You got a wife?"

"Yes, I do."

"You hate her so much you want to make her a widow? Seriously. Is that it?"

"Well, I'm not fighting with y'all about it," Jimmy said. "I don't fight with people who don't know what's good for them."

Jimmy threw his sack of campaign buttons up over his shoulder and walked on down the docks.

"We vote for DiCello here!" Hector called after him. "We're not stupid!"

"The hell with you, then!" Jimmy called back cheerfully.

Then Jimmy Moran stole a few beautiful Haitian mangos from a fruit display and dropped them into his jacket pocket. Jimmy had learned from Hispanics that Haitian mangos are the best for eating by hand, because their flesh is not stringy. Grafton's didn't usually have good fruit, but these were exceptional, gorgeous mangos, with minty green skins just turning a soft banana yellow. There were guys who had worked in the Bronx Terminal Vegetable Market for years and never tasted a fresh vegetable or fruit in their lives. It was sad, really. These were guys who would all die of heart attacks at fifty because they ate beef and bacon every day instead of the fruits and vegetables that were all over the place. Consider Hector's friend Ed, for example, sitting in front of a warehouse full of broccoli, eating *hamburgers*. A heart attack waiting to happen.

Jimmy Moran, on the other hand, ate everything, because he was in love with vegetables. His mother had always raised beautiful vegetables, and he would eat anything. He used to work as a crate stacker in a big cooler full of fresh herbs, and he would even eat parsley in bunches. He ate radishes and cauliflowers like they were apples. He would even take a small artichoke, peel off the tough outer leaves, and eat the rest of the artichoke whole and raw. He ate more vegetables than a hippie. People thought he was crazy.

On this night, he walked out of Grafton Brothers, eating Haitian mangos the Puerto Rican way. First, he massaged and squeezed the mango with his thumbs until the flesh was soft and pulpy beneath the skin. He worked the fruit with his thumbs until it had the consistency of jelly. Then he bit a small hole in the top and sucked out the insides. Sweet like coconut. Foreign-tasting, but nice.

In the next hours, Jimmy Moran campaigned through the wholesale houses of Dulrooney's, Evangelisti & Sons, DeRosa Importers, and E & M Wholesalers. He introduced himself to all the workers and made small talk with them. He talked to one poor fool who'd just spent his whole life's savings on a greyhound dog, and to another guy whose teenage daughter had cancer, and to a lucky son of a gun who was going on vacation to Bermuda. He talked to a whole lot of guys who told him he must be crazy to run for president against a mobbed-up animal like Joseph D. DiCello.

As he walked, he ate a handful of baby zucchini he'd stolen off a display at Evangelisti & Sons. Each zucchini was no longer than his littlest finger and tenderly flavorful in the sort of salty way that a big squash would never be. These were delicious raw, and the only kind of squash that didn't need any dip or sauce to have a flavor. Baby zucchinis were rare for the season, and expensive. He'd filled his pockets over at Evangelisti & Sons. A delicacy. He ate through them like they were peanuts.

At 4 A.M., he reached the bottom of his sack of campaign buttons. He was at a small, brand-new specialty gourmet house called Bella Foods, a place known to be very exclusive, which sold to the best restaurants in New York. He didn't think he would know anybody there at all, until he saw his old friend Casper Denni. They talked for a while about Jimmy's campaign and about their families. Casper also had a whole bunch of kids and an Italian wife. Casper had also been a porter for many years.

"Now, what happened? You had some kind of accident, I heard?" Casper said.

"The whole town's talkin'," Jimmy said. "Back surgery, buddy. What are you, a distributor now or something?"

Casper was sitting in a neat little white-painted booth, drinking a cup of coffee.

"No way," Casper said. "I got me a little business, selling coffee and replacement wheels for hand trucks."

"What?" Jimmy laughed.

"I'm serious, Jimmy. It's great."

"Get out of here."

"Check it out. Here's the idea. There are how many hand trucks at the market?"

"Hundreds. Millions."

"Thousands, Jimmy. Thousands. And every one of them a cheap piece of shit, as everybody knows. But every porter needs a hand truck, right? Because how many crates can one man carry alone?"

"Get out of here, Casper."

"One crate, right? Even a big monster like you, in your prime, you could only carry two crates, right? But with a hand truck, you can carry — what? — ten crates? Twelve crates, maybe? A hand truck is a very important tool, Mr. Moran, for the economic success of the individual."

"Excuse me, Casper? Excuse me, buddy, but who are you talking to here?"

"So, Mr. Moran, it's the middle of the night and your shitty hand truck pops a wheel. What do you do?"

"Find some other fool's hand truck and steal it."

"And get your head beat in? That's the old-fashioned way. Now you can just come to me. For five dollars, I sell you a new wheel. You give me another five dollars for a deposit on a hammer and wrench, which you get back when I get the tools back. Then I sell you a ten-cent cup of coffee for a buck, and I make six bucks out of the deal, and you have your hand truck fixed."

"Who would do that?"

"Everybody, Jimmy. Everybody comes to me now."

"In the last four months this happened?"

"I'm telling you, Jimmy. It's great. Tax-free. No union."

"You're something else, Casper. I tell you. You're really something else."

"You get to be old fucks like us, you need a new idea."

"I got an idea," Jimmy said, laughing. "I got a new idea. You make me your partner, buddy."

Casper laughed, too, and punched Jimmy in the arm.

"Listen," he said, "you ever work around this outfit before?"

"Around this place? No."

"You ever seen the mushroom man?"

"Casper," Jimmy said, "I don't know what you're talking about, buddy."

"You never saw the mushroom man? Oh, that's great. Oh, you gotta check this out, Jimmy. I can't believe you never heard about this guy. You want crazy? You want to see crazy? You just gotta check this guy out."

Casper came out from his neat little booth and led Jimmy into a huge refrigerated cooler warehouse.

"You're gonna love this guy, Jimmy."

They walked back to the end of the warehouse, and Casper stopped at a wide doorway, covered with the thick strips of plastic that keep temperatures even. A small refrigerated room. Casper pulled back a few of the plastic strips and stepped inside. He waved Jimmy to follow him, grinning like it would be a bordello in there.

Once inside, Jimmy Moran was faced with simply the finest mushroom produce he had ever seen in his life.

"Look at this booty, Jimmy," said Casper. "Have a look at this produce."

The crates were piled neatly, no higher than five to a stack, and the top crate of each stack was open for display. Right by the door was an open crate of snowy white button mushrooms, bigger than plums. There were crates of glossy shitake mushrooms, crates of shiny yellow straw mushrooms, and fresh porcini mushrooms that looked valuable enough to serve at God's table. Jimmy saw crates of portobellos as fleshy and thick as sirloin fillets. He saw a crate of wild black mushrooms, tiny and feathery like gills. He saw a crate of the kind of woody mushrooms his mother used to call toadstools, and also a crate of mushrooms that looked exactly like cauliflower heads. There were morels in the shapes and shades of coral. He saw a crate full of the tan, shelf-shaped mushrooms that grow out of rotting tree stumps. There were crates filled with Chinese mushrooms he could not name and other crates were filled with red- and blue-spotted mushrooms that may have been poisonous. The entire room smelled like damp manure, like the soil in a root cellar under a barn.

Jimmy Moran reached for a portobello mushroom, the biggest one he'd ever seen. He wanted it so much, but just as his hand touched it he heard a growl like an animal's. A huge and ugly man in overalls and a brown wool stocking cap was coming at him, exactly like a big dog.

Jimmy jumped back, startled, and Casper shoved him hard and shouted, "Get out! Get out!" Jimmy stumbled and fell backward out of the room, panicked. He fell through the plastic sheeting and landed hard on the concrete floor of the warehouse. Casper jumped out of the room after him, laughing and laughing.

Jimmy lay on his back on the cold floor and Casper said, "You're safe out here, Jimmy boy. Old mushroom man never comes out of there. Christ, what a crazy fucker. Don't touch the mushrooms, Jimmy. I should've told you don't touch the goddamn mushrooms unless you have permission."

On the floor, Jimmy tried to sit up, but his back spasmed, so he lay there for some time, willing his back to relax. Casper offered him a hand and Jimmy shook his head to refuse it.

"You okay, friend?" Casper said.

Jimmy nodded.

"Shit, you probably hurt your back. I forgot about your goddamn back. Jesus, I'm sorry."

Jimmy nodded again.

"That's a crazy fucker in there," Casper said, and again offered Jimmy his hand. Jimmy took it this time and very gingerly stood up. Casper parted the plastic strips and said, "Just look in there at that fucker."

Jimmy shook his head. He found that he was breathing very carefully.

"Come on. You don't have to go in there. Just look at that huge guy. He won't touch you if you leave the mushrooms alone. You got to take a good look at that guy."

Casper continued to insist, so Jimmy finally did poke his

head into the refrigerated mushroom room cautiously. The man in the room was indeed huge, and he stood quietly in the center. He was wearing brown overalls and he had a long brown beard. His feet were placed apart and his hands hung loosely fisted. Jimmy Moran and the mushroom man looked at each other. And while the man did not growl again, and while the man did not make any kind of a move forward, Jimmy Moran withdrew his head very slowly and stepped away from the door. He and Casper walked back to Casper's booth in the hallway.

Once they were out, Casper said, "The best mushrooms in the whole goddamn market."

Jimmy sat down on a crate next to Casper's booth and shut his eyes. His back was stiff. Sitting didn't help, so he stood again.

"The owner hired that crazy fucker a few months ago," Casper explained. "The guy used to be a trucker. He's from somewhere like Texas, or nobody knows where. They've got some kind of an arrangement, him and the owners. The guy never leaves the room. I sit here night after night, Jimmy, and I'm telling you, that crazy fucker never leaves the room. Those mushrooms, Jimmy, are honestly the best goddamn mushrooms you will ever see. The owners used to have a problem with people stealing the mushrooms, see."

"Jesus."

"No more problems with stealing anymore. I'll tell you that goddamn much. You plan on stealing these mushrooms, you gotta wrestle the big fella first."

"You have aspirin?" Jimmy asked.

"No, but I'll give you a cup of coffee, you pathetic bastard. Now get out of here, Jimmy. Feel better. Good luck on your election, even though I think you're a crazy bastard for running and I think somebody's probably going to put a bullet in your neck for you pretty soon. Now take your coffee and get out of here. Hurry up, or everyone will think I'm giving the stuff away for free. Everyone will think I can't even run my own goddamn business."

Jimmy Moran walked slowly through the complicated and connecting parking lots to find his car. He swung his arms as he walked, trying to take the stiffness out of his back. He thought that he probably looked like an idiot doing this, but he didn't care. As it turned out, he was walking along the back parking lot of the Korean market most of the time anyway, and he didn't care what Koreans thought of how he looked. The Korean market was huge now. Jimmy Moran thought that someday the Koreans might take over the entire Bronx Terminal Vegetable Market, an idea he wasn't crazy about in any way. The Koreans worked ridiculous hours and didn't even have a union. They sold vegetables nobody had ever even heard of.

He was tired. During his four months off, he'd been keeping human hours for the first time in his adult life — asleep during the darkness and awake during the day — and he was not yet readjusted to being up in the middle of the night. It was nearly dawn. It took him almost an hour to get back to where he had parked, under a strong streetlight. His car did look beautiful. He loved his car. On this cloudy and damp night, under this big artificial beam of light, it looked like some kind of a sea animal — watery blue and powerful, with shimmering fins. The taillights looked like reflective decoy eyes.

He had a second sack of campaign buttons in the trunk of his car. His plan was to drive to the north side of the market and hand out buttons at some of the bigger commercial houses over there before everyone left for the day. He drove toward the north, passing the lines and lines of freight trucks all backed up against dark loading docks. The cabs of the trucks were dim and closed. The drivers, mostly Southerners like himself, slept inside on hidden mattresses while the porters loaded the freight.

Men pushed hand trucks loaded with crates and maneuvered along the narrow alleys between the big trucks. Sometimes the men would pause and give Jimmy Moran a thumbs-up gesture for his beautiful car. Sometimes they would come jogging across his path, concentrating on their destination, and he would nearly hit them.

Jimmy came upon a security guard he knew, patrolling a parking lot on foot. Low, thick diesel fumes reached up past the man's knees, making it look like he was wading in mist. Jimmy stopped to talk. The guard was a friendly Polack from Jimmy's own neighborhood named Paul Gadomski. Jimmy rolled down his window and Paul leaned against the Chrysler and lit a cigarette.

"What is this, a 'fifty-eight?" Paul asked.

"It's a 'fifty-six, Pauly."

"She's a sweetheart."

"Thanks. Have a button," Jimmy said, and handed a campaign button out of the window.

"What's this? You're not running against DiCello?"

"I am," Jimmy said. Christ, he was tired. "And I'd like to think I can count on your vote, Paul."

"Hell, I'm not voting in your union, Jim. Get serious. I'm no teamster. I'm a cop."

"*You* get serious, Pauly. You're no cop, buddy."

"Same thing."

"Security guard?"

"Well, I'm damn sure no teamster."

"I'd sure like it if you'd wear the button anyhow."

"Hell, Jim. I can't wear no teamster's campaign button on my uniform."

"Well, think it over, Pauly."

"I'll bring it home for my kid to play with," Paul said. He put the button in his jacket pocket.

The two men, alone in a back parking lot, talked about

business. Paul said that when Jimmy was out for back surgery, there was a trucker who got his neck slit one night. Nobody had been arrested for it yet. Jimmy said he hadn't heard about that. Paul said the corpse had been found underneath some other driver's truck. *That* driver, some guy who was hauling bananas all the way up from Florida, claimed he didn't know anything about any murder, so the police let him go. Paul couldn't believe how gullible the cops were. Paul said the cops didn't seem too interested in finding out what really happened that night. Jimmy said that it was almost always that way, because the cops were usually mobbed-up and corrupt like everyone else. Paul said he knew for a fact that the murdered guy had hit the Trifecta that very afternoon and had been bragging all night about making something like twenty grand. Paul said there was crazy bullshit all over the market for about a week, what with the cops sealing off areas and asking all the wrong questions. Jimmy said it sounded to him like the murder had been a fight over a parking spot, and he would be suspicious of the banana-truck driver from Florida. Jimmy recalled that the first year he'd ever worked at the market, he'd seen a guy beaten to death with a tire iron over a parking spot dispute. Jimmy had seen lots of parking spot disputes turn violent.

Paul said that it was just a bunch of fucking animals working at this place. Jimmy agreed, and the two men said good night.

Jimmy Moran drove on. He passed a handsome fleet of refrigerated supermarket trucks, loading in at Bennetti & Perke, the major corporate wholesaler that distributed to all the big Eastern seaboard supermarket chains. Jimmy didn't know who owned Bennetti & Perke, but it was definitely a very, very rich man, who was probably asleep somewhere in a big house right on the ocean.

There was so much fortune being shuffled around every

night here at the Bronx Terminal Vegetable Market, it was almost unbelievable. It would be unbelievable and unimaginable to those who had not seen the place at work. The hurricane fences and razor-wire coils and security floodlights gave the market the look of a prison, but it was certainly no prison, as Jimmy and everyone who had ever worked there knew. It was no prison. It was, actually, a *bank*.

When Jimmy Moran was just a young porter, he and his buddies had wasted a lot of time trying to figure out how to skim off some of that fortune. They'd wasted a lot of time trying to imagine how much money was passed around every night at the market. That was a young man's game, of course. It was the old men who understood there was never a way to steal any real money unless you were already rich.

The summer earlier, Jimmy's oldest son, Danny, had worked part-time at Grafton Brothers as a porter. Danny had tried in the same lazy way to figure out how much money was contained in the market and how to get his hands on it. Jimmy was aware of this. Danny also wanted to know how to steal it, how to hoist it, how to skim it. On their drive home together in the early morning, Danny would speculate aimlessly about money. Wouldn't it be fantastic, Danny would say, to skim even one lousy cent off every pound of produce sold at the market in one night? How much money would that be a week? A month? A year? Wouldn't it even be *fair* to be able to skim a little off the top? Considering how hard porters worked, and for such a shitty pay?

"You don't know what you're talking about," Jimmy would tell his son. "Just forget about it."

"What about the Korean market?" Danny asked. "All their deals are in cash. You could just mug one of those guys and get a fortune. All those Korean guys are carrying around at least five grand all the time."

"No, Danny. Nobody carries that kind of cash."

"Koreans do. Koreans are scared of banks."

"You don't know what you're talking about."

"That's what the truckers say."

"Then you can be damn sure you don't know what you're talking about."

Of course it was ridiculous to think about stealing money from anybody here, because a lot of people carried guns and knives. People were always killing each other over *nothing*, just to pass the time. It was ridiculous to think about all the money other people made here. It would give you chest pains, just thinking about it.

Jimmy had meant to park at Bennetti & Perke. He'd thought it was a good place to hand out his second bag of campaign buttons, but now he wasn't so sure. His back was really bothering him, and he wasn't sure how he was supposed to carry the heavy sack. For that matter, he wasn't sure how he was supposed to go back to work as a porter in just two days, as he was scheduled to. How was he supposed to haul crates of fruits and vegetables around? How was he supposed to do that? Honestly, how?

So Jimmy Moran drove on. It was after 5:30 A.M., and his back was seriously hurting. He circled around Bennetti & Perke and then headed out of the market altogether. He would just go home. He would just forget about campaigning. As he drove, he thought for the first time in ages about his old friend Martin O'Ryan.

From March of 1981 to January of 1982, Jimmy had worked as a buyer on a trial basis for a discount greengrocery chain called Apple Paradise. It was a big opportunity for advancement, and his old friend Martin O'Ryan had gotten him the job. It was quite a promotion, to be taken off the docks and made a buyer.

Buyers got to work in offices up above the actual market, and buyers could really prosper.

Jimmy's friend Martin O'Ryan had actually been very good at buying. He was a maniac at telephone deals, really fierce at negotiating with truckers, farmers, importers, and distributors for the best price. Martin made a lot of money for Apple Paradise and for himself that year.

"Whaddaya got?!" Martin would shout into the phone. "I need iceberg! . . . Twenty-five dollars? Fuck you, twenty-five dollars! I'll take it for eighteen! . . . Give me eighteen or I'll come over and burn down your motherfucking *house!* . . . Give me eighteen or I'll rip your motherfucking *lungs* out! . . . Give me eighteen or I'll *blind* you and I'll personally come to your house myself and I will blind your — okay, I'll take it for twenty."

Then Martin would hang up the phone and start with someone else.

Martin O'Ryan and Jimmy Moran were put in the same office, at desks across from each other. They were best friends. Martin was the first friend Jimmy ever made when he came up from Virginia with his mom as a twelve-year-old hillbilly kid. Jimmy and Martin had started off as porters together and joined the union together and been to each other's weddings. He loved Martin, but he couldn't concentrate on his own telephone deals with Martin shouting across the room from him. ("Get me that truck of potatoes, you worthless fuck, you worthless, lying cocksucker fuckhole, or I'll rape you personally *myself!*")

Martin was the nicest guy in the world, but it was distracting. At the end of the year, Martin got a huge bonus and an official job for the company, and Jimmy did not. It worked out fine, in the end. Jimmy found another job quickly enough, working on the loading docks as a porter again.

Martin was honestly one of the nicest guys in the world, and

Martin and Jimmy loved each other, but they hadn't seen each other for quite a while.

Jimmy needed to gas up the Chrysler and he knew that the small gas station in his neighborhood wouldn't be open yet, so he didn't take his usual exit toward home. Instead, he kept on driving around, looking for a twenty-four-hour service station, and that is how he eventually ended up on Route 95.

He was familiar with that highway. Back in the middle of the 1980s, he'd worked for a while as a delivery driver for a small gourmet vegetable wholesale company called Parthenon Produce, run by two Greeks. This was the nicest job he'd ever had. He used to deliver quality greens — mostly arugula and watercress — from the Bronx Terminal Vegetable Market, up Route 95, to all the fancy stores along Long Island Sound and up into Connecticut as far as Ridgefield. It was a long drive but pleasant, and he used to get into Ridgefield (a place he and Gina used to call "Rich-field") around eight or nine in the morning, when the wealthy men were just heading off to their jobs.

He had liked that delivery job. He had been happy with that job, but the two Greeks had sold their business in 1985. They'd offered him a chance to buy that particular delivery route as his own, but Jimmy Moran just didn't have that kind of money at the time.

Jimmy Moran drove past New Rochelle and Mount Vernon and into Connecticut. It was very early in the morning, and a clear day. As he drove, Jimmy thought that if he could have made more money at the Bronx Terminal Vegetable Market, he would have moved his wife and all his kids up to Connecticut long ago. They still talked about it all the time: the broad lawns, the quiet schools, the tall wives. Jimmy Moran's brother Patrick, ironically enough, had married Gina's sister Louisa, and those two had moved to Connecticut right away. But Patrick and

Louisa, of course, didn't have any kids, and it was easier for them to move. They had moved to Danbury, and they had a pretty nice little place, with a patio.

Gina's sister Louisa used to be a genuinely sexy girl when she was a teenager. She was famous around the neighborhood for being no good in a very fun way, and Jimmy Moran's brother Patrick had always been crazy about Louisa Lisante. But Jimmy had always preferred Gina. In the summer of 1970, when Jimmy had his first job as a porter at the market, he would see Gina and Louisa Lisante waiting for the bus together every morning when he got home from work. They always wore shorts and sandals. They were setting off for their summer jobs as waitresses near the beach. Jimmy used to steal beautiful ripe Holland tomatoes from the market and leave them on the Lisantes' doorstep as paperweights for little love notes to Gina: *I love Gina . . . Gina is pretty . . . Gina has pretty legs . . . I wish Gina would marry me.*

Jimmy thought about Gina and Patrick and Louisa as he drove all the way into Ridgefield, Connecticut. Although he had not planned it this way, his timing on this particular morning was the same as his timing with the Parthenon Produce delivery route, and he arrived in Ridgefield just as the men of the town were leaving for work. It was nearly ten years since he had been to Ridgefield. In the old days, when he was finished with his route, he used to drive around the most affluent neighborhoods, studying the houses. These homes had all seemed so confidently undefended to him, and he had felt traces of a young man's desire to rob them. Of course, it was not the contents of the houses he had wanted but the houses themselves. Particularly the large stone houses.

The house that Jimmy Moran had always particularly really wanted was absolutely huge. It was a half-mile from the center of Ridgefield — a great slate-roof manor on top of a steep hill, with a circular driveway and white columns. He used to drive up to this exact house some early mornings when the gourmet greens were all delivered. His three-ton Parthenon Produce delivery truck would rumble obnoxiously up the grade each time he downshifted. In all those mornings, he never once saw anybody, or any car, anywhere near that house. It always seemed like such a crime to have such a huge house sitting there empty. It was such a well-kept empty house, and Jimmy used to consider simply moving in. What if he could do that? What if he could simply take it over? He would think: *Imagine what all my kids could do with all the room in that big house.*

On this morning, he parked his Chrysler across the road from the house, which had not changed as far as he could see. He had stopped in Stamford to fill the tank with gas and had purchased a bottle of aspirin at a convenience store there. Christ, his back hurt! How was he supposed to go back to the docks in only two days? Honestly, how?

Jimmy opened the bottle and ate a handful of aspirins — chewed and swallowed without water. It was a well-known fact that a chewed aspirin, while disgusting to the taste, would act faster than a whole aspirin, which would sit intact and useless for some time in a person's stomach acid. He ate several aspirins and he thought about his wedding night. He was just nineteen years old then, and Gina was even younger.

She had asked him on their wedding night, "How many kids do you want to have, Jimmy?"

He'd said, "Your boobs will get bigger whenever you're pregnant, right?"

"I think so."

"Then I'll take ten or eleven kids, Gina," he had said.

In fact, they ended up having six, which was ridiculous enough. Six kids! And Jimmy in the produce business! What had they been *thinking?* They'd had three boys and three girls. The girls had Italian names and the boys had Irish names, a cornball little gimmick that was Jimmy's idea. Six kids!

The pain in Jimmy's back, which had started as stiffness and turned to cramps, was stoked up even higher now. It was a terrible pain, localized at the point of his recent surgery, emphasized periodically by a hot pulse that shook his body like a sob. He emptied some more of the aspirins from the bottle into his palm and he looked at the big house. He thought about his grandfather who had shot through the engine of a company coal truck, and he thought about his uncle who'd got assassinated by company detectives for organizing, and he thought about the black lung. He thought about his doctors and about Joseph D. DiCello and about the mushroom man and about Hector the Haitian distributor and about his brother Patrick, who he rarely saw anymore at all because Connecticut was so far.

He chewed the aspirins and counted the windows of the great house across the road. Jimmy Moran had never thought to count the windows before. He worked the bits of aspirin out of his teeth with his tongue and counted thirty-two windows. Thirty-two windows that he could see, just from the road! He thought and thought and then he spoke.

"Even for me, with six kids and a wife . . ." Jimmy supposed aloud. "Even for me, with six kids and a wife, it must be a sin to have such a house. That must be it."

Jimmy Moran thought and thought, but this was the best he could figure. This was all he could come up with.

"Even for me," he said again, "it must be a sin."

The Famous
Torn and Restored Lit
Cigarette Trick

✦   ✦   ✦

IN HUNGARY, Richard Hoffman's family had been the
manufacturers of Hoffman's Rose Water, a product which
was used at the time for both cosmetic and medicinal pur-
poses. Hoffman's mother drank the rose water for her indiges-
tion, and his father used it to scent and cool his groin after
exercise. The servants rinsed the Hoffmans' table linens in a
cold bath infused with rose water such that even the kitchen
would be perfumed. The cook mixed a dash of it into her
sweetbread batter. For evening events, Budapest ladies wore
expensive imported colognes, but Hoffman's Rose Water was a
staple product of daytime hygiene for all women, as requisite as
soap. Hungarian men could be married for decades without
ever realizing that the natural smell of their wives' skin was not,
in fact, a refined scent of blooming roses.

Richard Hoffman's father was a perfect gentleman, but his
mother slapped the servants. His paternal grandfather had been
a drunk and a brawler, and his maternal grandfather had been a

Bavarian boar hunter, trampled to death at the age of ninety by his own horses. After her husband died of consumption, Hoffman's mother transferred the entirety of the family's fortune into the hands of a handsome Russian charlatan named Katanovsky, a common conjurer and a necromancer who promised Madame Hoffman audiences with the dead. As for Richard Hoffman himself, he moved to America, where he murdered two people.

Hoffman immigrated to Pittsburgh during World War II and worked as a busboy for over a decade. He had a terrible, humiliating way of speaking with customers.

"I am from Hungary!" he would bark. "Are you Hungary, too? If you Hungary, you in the right place!"

For years he spoke such garbage, even after he had learned excellent English, and could be mistaken for a native-born steelworker. With this ritual degradation he was tipped generously, and saved enough money to buy a supper club called the Pharaoh's Palace, featuring a nightly magic act, a comic, and some showgirls. It was very popular with gamblers and the newly rich.

When Hoffman was in his late forties, he permitted a young man named Ace Douglas to audition for a role as a supporting magician. Ace had no nightclub experience, no professional photos or references, but he had a beautiful voice over the telephone, and Hoffman granted him an audience.

On the afternoon of the audition, Ace arrived in a tuxedo. His shoes had a wealthy gleam, and he took his cigarettes from a silver case, etched with his clean initials. He was a slim, attractive man with fair brown hair. When he was not smiling, he looked like a matinee idol, and when he was smiling, he looked like a friendly lifeguard. Either way, he seemed altogether too affable to perform good magic (Hoffman's other magicians cultivated an intentional menace), but his act was wonderful and entertaining, and he was unsullied by the often stupid fashions of magic at the time. (Ace didn't claim to be descended from a vampire, for instance, or empowered with secrets from the tomb of Ramses, or to have been kidnaped by Gypsies as a child, or raised by missionaries in the mysterious Orient.) He didn't even have a female assistant, unlike Hoffman's other magicians, who knew that some bounce in fishnets could save any sloppy act. What's more, Ace had the good sense and class not to call himself the Great anything or the Magnificent anybody.

Onstage, with his smooth hair and white gloves, Ace Douglas had the sexual ease of Sinatra.

There was an older waitress known as Big Sandra at the Pharaoh's Palace on the afternoon of Ace Douglas's audition, setting up the cocktail bar. She watched the act for a few minutes, then approached Hoffman, and whispered in his ear, "At night, when I'm all alone in my bed, I sometimes think about men."

"I bet you do, Sandra," said Hoffman.

She was always talking like this. She was a fantastic, dirty woman, and he had actually had sex with her a few times.

She whispered, "And when I get to thinking about men, Hoffman, I think about a man exactly like that."

"You like him?" Hoffman asked.

"Oh, my."

"You think the ladies will like him?"

"Oh, my," said Big Sandra, fanning herself daintily. "Heavens, yes."

Hoffman fired his other two magicians within the hour.

After that, Ace Douglas worked every night that the Pharaoh's Palace was open. He was the highest paid performer in Pittsburgh. This was not during a decade when nice young women generally came to bars unescorted, but the Pharaoh's Palace became a place where nice women — extremely attractive young single nice women — would come with their best girlfriends and their best dresses to watch the Ace Douglas magic show. And men would come to the Pharaoh's Palace to watch the nice young women and to buy them expensive cocktails.

Hoffman had his own table at the back of the restaurant, and after the magic show was over, he and Ace Douglas would entertain young ladies there. The girls would blindfold Ace, and Hoffman would choose an object on the table for him to identify.

"It's a fork," Ace would say. "It's a gold cigarette lighter."

The more suspicious girls would open their purses and seek unusual objects — family photographs, prescription medicine, a traffic ticket — all of which Ace would describe easily. The girls would laugh, and doubt his blindfold, and cover his eyes with their damp hands. They had names like Lettie and Pearl and Siggie and Donna. They all loved dancing, and they all tended to keep their nice fur wraps with them at the table, out of pride. Hoffman would introduce them to eligible or otherwise interested businessmen. Ace Douglas would escort the nice young ladies to the parking lot late at night, listening politely as they spoke up to him, resting his hand reassuringly on the small of their backs if they wavered.

At the end of every evening, Hoffman would say sadly, "Me and Ace, we see so many girls come and go . . ."

Ace Douglas could turn a pearl necklace into a white glove and a cigarette lighter into a candle. He could produce a silk scarf from a lady's hairpin. But his finest trick was in 1959, when he produced his little sister from a convent school and offered her to Richard Hoffman in marriage.

Her name was Angela. She had been a volleyball champion in the convent school, and she had legs like a movie star's legs, and a very pretty laugh. She was ten days pregnant on her wedding day, although she and Hoffman had known each other for only two weeks. Shortly thereafter, Angela had a daughter, and they named her Esther. Throughout the early 1960s, they all prospered happily.

Esther turned eight years old, and the Hoffmans celebrated her birthday with a special party at the Pharaoh's Palace. That night, there was a thief sitting in the cocktail lounge.

He didn't look like a thief. He was dressed well enough, and he was served without any trouble. The thief drank a few martinis. Then, in the middle of the magic show, he leaped over the bar, kicked the bartender away, punched the cash register open, and ran out of the Pharaoh's Palace with his hands full of tens and twenties.

The customers were screaming, and Hoffman heard it from the kitchen. He chased the thief into the parking lot and caught him by the hair.

"You steal from me?" he yelled. "You fucking steal from me?"

"Back off, pal," the thief said. The thief's name was George Purcell, and he was drunk.

"You fucking steal from me?" Hoffman yelled.

He shoved George Purcell into the side of a yellow Buick. Some of the customers had come outside, and were watching from the doorway of the restaurant. Ace Douglas came out, too. He walked past the customers, into the parking lot, and lit a cigarette. Ace Douglas watched as Hoffman lifted the thief by his shirt and threw him against the hood of a Cadillac.

"Back off me!" Purcell said.

"You fucking steal from me?"

"You ripped my shirt!" Purcell cried, aghast. He was looking down at his ripped shirt when Hoffman shoved him into the side of the yellow Buick again.

Ace Douglas said, "Richard? Could you take it easy?" (The

Buick was his, and it was new. Hoffman was steadily pounding George Purcell's head into the door.) "Richard? Excuse me? Excuse me, Richard. Please don't damage my car, Richard."

Hoffman dropped the thief to the ground and sat on his chest. He caught his breath and smiled. "Don't ever," he explained, "ever. Don't ever steal from me."

Still sitting on Purcell's chest, he calmly picked up the tens and twenties that had fallen on the asphalt and handed them to Ace Douglas. Then he slid his hand into Purcell's back pocket and pulled out a wallet, which he opened. He took nine dollars from the wallet, because that was all the money he found there. Purcell was indignant.

"That's my money!" he shouted. "You can't take my money!"

"*Your* money?" Hoffman slapped Purcell's head. "*Your* money? *Your* fucking money?"

Ace Douglas tapped Hoffman's shoulder lightly and said, "Richard? Excuse me? Let's just wait for the police, okay? How about it, Richard?"

"*Your* money?" Hoffman was slapping Purcell in the face now with the wallet. "You fucking steal from me, you have no money! You fucking steal from me, I own all your money!"

"Aw, Jesus," Purcell said. "Quit it, will ya? Leave me alone, will ya?"

"Let him be," Ace Douglas said.

"*Your* money? I own all your money!" Hoffman bellowed. "I own you! You fucking steal from me, I own your fucking *shoes!*"

Hoffman lifted Purcell's leg and pulled off one of his shoes. It was a nice brown leather wingtip. He hit Purcell with it once in the face and tore off the other shoe. He beat on Purcell a few times with that shoe until he lost his appetite for it. Then he just sat on Purcell's chest for a while, catching his breath, hugging the shoes and rocking in a sad way.

"Aw, Jesus," Purcell groaned. His lip was bleeding.

"Let's get up now, Richard," Ace suggested.

After some time, Hoffman jumped off Purcell and walked back into the Pharaoh's Palace, carrying the thief's shoes. His tuxedo was torn in one knee, and his shirt was hanging loose. The customers backed against the walls of the restaurant and let him pass. He went into the kitchen and threw Purcell's shoes into one of the big garbage cans next to the potwashing sinks. He went into his office and shut the door.

The potwasher was a young Cuban fellow named Manuel. He picked George Purcell's brown wingtips out of the garbage can and held one of them up against the bottom of his own foot. It seemed to be a good match, so he took off his own shoes and put on Purcell's. Manuel's shoes were plastic sandals, and these he threw away. A little later, Manuel watched with satisfaction as the chef dumped a vat of cold gravy on top of the sandals, and when he went back to washing pots, he whistled to himself a little song of good luck.

A policeman arrived. He handcuffed George Purcell and brought him into Hoffman's office. Ace Douglas followed them.

"You want to press charges?" the cop asked.

"No," Hoffman said. "Forget about it."

"You don't press charges, I have to let him go."

"Let him go."

"This man says you took his shoes."

"He's a criminal. He came in my restaurant with no shoes."

"He took my shoes," Purcell said. His shirt collar was soaked with blood.

"He never had no shoes on. Look at him. No shoes on his feet."

"You took my money and my goddamn shoes, you animal. Twenty-dollar shoes!"

"Get this stealing man out of my restaurant, please," Hoffman said.

"Officer?" Ace Douglas said. "Excuse me, but I was here the

whole time, and this man never did have any shoes on. He's a derelict, sir."

"But I'm wearing dress socks!" Purcell shouted. "Look at me! Look at me!"

Hoffman stood up and walked out of his office. The cop followed Hoffman, leading George Purcell. Ace Douglas trailed behind. On his way through the restaurant, Hoffman stopped to pick up his daughter, Esther, from her birthday party. He carried her out to the parking lot.

"Listen to me now," he told Purcell. "You ever steal from me again, I'll kill you."

"Take it easy," the cop said.

"If I even see you on the street, I'll fucking kill you."

The cop said, "You want to press charges, pal, you press charges. Otherwise, you take it easy."

"He doesn't like to be robbed," Ace Douglas explained.

"Animal," Purcell muttered.

"You see this little girl?" Hoffman asked. "My little girl is eight years old today. If I'm walking on the street with my little girl and I see you, I will leave her on one side of the street and I will cross the street and I will kill you in front of my little girl."

"That's enough," the cop said. He led George Purcell out of the parking lot and took off his handcuffs.

The cop and the thief walked away together. Hoffman stood on the steps of the Pharaoh's Palace, holding Esther and shouting. "Right in front of my little girl, you make me kill you? What kind of man are you? Crazy man! You ruin a little girl's life! Terrible man!"

Esther was crying. Ace Douglas took her from Hoffman's arms.

The next week, the thief George Purcell came back to the Pharaoh's Palace. It was noon, and very quiet. The prep cook was making chicken stock, and Manuel the potwasher was cleaning out the dry goods storage area. Hoffman was in his office, ordering vegetables from his wholesaler. Purcell came straight back into the kitchen, sober.

"I want my goddamn shoes!" he yelled, pounding on the office door. "Twenty-dollar shoes!"

Then Richard Hoffman came out of his office and beat George Purcell to death with a meat mallet. Manuel the potwasher tried to hold him back, and Hoffman beat him to death with the meat mallet, too.

Esther Hoffman did not grow up to be a natural magician. Her hands were dull. It was no fault of her own, just an unfortunate birth flaw. Otherwise, she was a bright girl.

Her uncle, Ace Douglas, had been the American champion close-up magician for three years running. He'd won his titles using no props or tools at all, except a single silver dollar coin. During one competition, he'd vanished and produced the coin for fifteen dizzying minutes without the expert panel of judges ever noticing that the coin spent a lot of time resting openly on Ace Douglas's knee. He would put it there, where it lay gleaming to be seen if one of the judges had only glanced away for a moment from Ace's hands. But they would never glance away, convinced that he still held a coin before them in his fingers. They were not fools, but they were dupes for his fake takes, his fake drops, his mock passes, and a larger cast of impossible moves so deceptive they went entirely unnoticed. Ace Douglas had motions he himself had never even named. He was a scholar of misdirection. He proscribed skepticism. His fingers were as loose and quick as thoughts.

But Esther Hoffman's magic was sadly pedestrian. She did the Famous Dancing Cane trick, the Famous Vanishing Milk trick, and the Famous Interlocking Chinese Rings trick. She produced parakeets from light bulbs and pulled a dove from a burning pan. She performed at birthday parties and could float a child. She performed at grammar schools and could cut and restore the neckties of principals. If the principal was a lady, Esther could borrow a ring from the principal's finger, lose it, and then find it in a child's pocket. If the lady principal wore no jewelry, Esther could simply run a sword through the woman's neck while the children in the audience screamed in spasms of rapture.

Simple, artless tricks.

"You're young," Ace told her. "You'll improve."

But she did not. Esther made more money giving flute lessons to little girls than performing magic. She was a fine flutist, and this was maddening to her. Why all this worthless musical skill?

"Your fingers are very quick," Ace told her. "There's nothing wrong with your fingers. But it's not about quickness, Esther. You don't have to speed through coins."

"I hate coins."

"You should handle coins as if they amuse you, Esther. Not as if they frighten you."

"With coins, it's like I'm wearing oven mitts."

"Coins are not always easy."

"I never fool anybody. I can't misdirect."

"It's not about misdirection, Esther. It's about *direction*."

"I don't have hands," Esther complained. "I have paws."

It was true that Esther could only fumble coins and cards, and she would never be a deft magician. She had no gift. Also, she hadn't the poise. Esther had seen photographs of her uncle when he was young at the Pharaoh's Palace, leaning against patrician pillars of marble in his tuxedo and cufflinks. No form of magic existed that was close-up enough for him. He could sit on a chair surrounded on all sides by the biggest goons of spectators — people who challenged him or grabbed his arm in mid-pass — and he would borrow from a goon some common object and absolutely vanish it. Some goon's car keys in Ace's hand would turn into absolutely nothing. Absolutely gone.

Ace's nightclub act at the Pharaoh's Palace had been a tribute to the elegant vices: coins, cards, dice, champagne flutes, and cigarettes. Everything was to suggest and encourage drinking, sin, gamesmanship, and money. The fluidity of fortune. He could do a whole act of cigarette effects alone, starting with a single cigarette borrowed from a lady in the audience. He would pass it through a coin and give the coin to the lady. He would tear the cigarette in half and restore it, swallow it, cough it back up along with six more, duplicate them, and duplicate them again until he ended up with lit cigarettes smoking hot between all his fingers and in his mouth, behind his ears, emerging from every pocket — surprised? he was terrified! — and then, with a nod, all the lit cigarettes would vanish except the original. That one he would smoke luxuriously during the applause.

Also, Esther had pictures of her father during the same period, when he owned the Pharaoh's Palace. He was handsome in his tuxedo, but with a heavy posture. She had inherited his thick wrists.

When Richard Hoffman got out of prison, he moved in with Ace and Esther. Ace had a tremendous home in the country by then, a tall yellow Victorian house with a mile of woods behind it and a lawn like a baron's. Ace Douglas had made a tidy fortune from magic. He had operated the Pharaoh's Palace from the time that Hoffman was arrested, and, with Hoffman's permission, had eventually sold it at great profit to a gourmet restaurateur. Esther had been living with Ace since she'd finished high school, and she had a whole floor to herself. Ace's little sister Angela had divorced Hoffman, also with his permission, and had moved to Florida to live with her new husband. What Hoffman had never permitted was for Esther to visit him in prison, and so it had been fourteen years since they'd seen each other. In prison he had grown even sturdier. He seemed shorter than Ace and Esther remembered, and some weight gained had made him more broad. He had also grown a thick beard, with handsome red tones. He was easily moved to tears, or, at least, seemed to be always on the verge of being moved to tears. The first few weeks of living together again were not altogether comfortable for Esther and Hoffman. They had only the briefest conversations, such as this one:

Hoffman asked Esther, "How old are you now?"

"Twenty-two."

"I've got undershirts older than you."

Or, in another conversation, Hoffman said, "The fellows I met in prison are the nicest fellows in the world."

And Esther said, "Actually, Dad, they probably aren't."

And so on.

In December of that year, Hoffman attended a magic show of Esther's, performed at a local elementary school.

"She's really not very good," he reported later to Ace.

"I think she's fine," Ace said. "She's fine for the kids, and she enjoys herself."

"She's pretty terrible. Too dramatic."

"Perhaps."

"She says, BEHOLD! It's terrible. BEHOLD this! BEHOLD that!"

"But they're children." Ace said. "With children, you need to explain when you're about to do a trick and when you just did one, because they're so excited they don't realize what's going on. They don't even know what a magician is. They can't tell the difference between when you're doing magic and when you're just standing there."

"I think she's very nervous."

"Could be."

"She says, BEHOLD THE PARAKEET!"

"Her parakeet tricks are not bad."

"It's not dignified," Hoffman said. "She convinces nobody."

"It's not meant to be dignified, Richard. It's for the children."

The next week, Hoffman bought Esther a large white rabbit.

"If you do the tricks for the children, you should have a rabbit," he told her.

Esther hugged him. She said, "I've never had a rabbit."

Hoffman lifted the rabbit from the cage. It was an unnaturally enormous rabbit.

"Is it pregnant?" Esther asked.

"No, she is not. She is only large."

"That's an extremely large rabbit for any magic trick," Ace observed.

Esther said, "They haven't invented the hat big enough to pull that rabbit out of."

"She actually folds up to a small size," Hoffman said. He held the rabbit between his hands as if she were an accordion and squeezed her into a great white ball.

"She seems to like that," Ace said, and Esther laughed.

"She doesn't mind it. Her name is Bonnie." Hoffman held the rabbit forward by the nape of her neck, as though she were a massive kitten. Dangling fully stretched like that, she was bigger than a big raccoon.

"Where'd you get her?" Esther asked.

"From the newspaper!" Hoffman announced, beaming.

Esther liked Bonnie the rabbit more than she liked her trick doves and parakeets, who were attractive enough but were essentially only pigeons that had been lucky with their looks. Ace liked Bonnie, too. He allowed Bonnie to enjoy the entirety of his large Victorian home, with little regard for her pellets, which were small, rocky, and inoffensive. She particularly enjoyed sitting in the center of the kitchen table, and from that spot would regard Ace, Esther, and Hoffman gravely. In this manner, Bonnie was very feline.

"Will she always be this judgmental?" Esther asked.

Bonnie became more canine when she was allowed outdoors. She would sleep on the porch, lying on her side in a patch of sun, and if anyone approached the porch she would look up at that person lazily, in the manner of a bored and trustful dog. At night, she slept with Hoffman. He tended to sleep on his side, curled like a child, and Bonnie would sleep upon him, perched on his highest point, which was generally his hip.

As a performer, however, Bonnie was useless. She was far too large to be handled gracefully onstage, and on the one occasion that Esther did try to produce her from a hat, she hung in the air so sluggishly that the children in the back rows were sure that she was a fake. She appeared to be a huge toy, as store-bought as their own stuffed animals.

"Bonnie will never be a star," Hoffman said.

Ace said, "You spoiled her, Richard, the way the magicians have been spoiling their lovely assistants for decades. You spoiled Bonnie by sleeping with her."

That spring, a young lawyer and his wife (who was also a young lawyer) moved into the large Victorian house next door to Ace Douglas's large Victorian house. It all happened very swiftly. The widow who had lived there for decades died in her sleep, and the place was sold within a few weeks. The new neighbors had great ambitions. The husband, whose name was Ronald Wilson, telephoned Ace and asked whether there were any problems he should know about in the area, regarding water-drainage patterns or frost heaves. Ronald had plans for a garden and was interested in building an arbor to extend from the back of the house. His wife, whose name was Ruth-Ann, was running for probate judge of the county. Ronald and Ruth-Ann were tall and had perfect manners. They had no children.

Three days after the Wilsons moved in next door, Bonnie the rabbit disappeared. She was on the porch, and then she was not.

Hoffman searched all afternoon for Bonnie. On Esther's recommendation, he spent that evening walking up and down the road with a flashlight, looking to see if Bonnie had been hit by a car. The next day, he walked through the woods behind the house, calling the rabbit for hours. He left a bowl of cut vegetables on the porch, with some fresh water. Several times during the night, Hoffman got up to see whether Bonnie was on the porch, eating the food. Eventually, he just wrapped himself in blankets and lay down on the porch swing, keeping a vigil beside the vegetables. He slept out there for a week, changing the food every morning and evening, to keep the scent fresh.

Esther made a poster with a drawing of Bonnie (which looked very much like a spaniel in her rendering) and a caption reading: LARGE RABBIT MISSING. She stapled copies of the poster on telephone poles throughout town and placed a notice in the newspaper. Hoffman wrote a letter to the neighbors, Ronald and Ruth-Ann Wilson, and slid it under their door. The letter described Bonnie's color and weight, gave the date and time of her disappearance, and requested any information on the subject at all. The Wilsons did not call with news, so the next day Hoffman went over to their house and rang the doorbell. Ronald Wilson answered.

"Did you get my letter?" Hoffman asked.

"About the rabbit?" Ronald said. "Have you found him?"

"The rabbit is a girl. And the rabbit belongs to my daughter. She was a gift. Have you seen her?"

"She didn't get in the road, did she?"

"Is Bonnie in your house, Mr. Wilson?"

"Is Bonnie the rabbit's name?"

"Yes."

"How would Bonnie get in our house?"

"Perhaps you have some broken window in the basement?"

"You think she's in our basement?"

"Have you looked for her in your basement?"

"No."

"Can I look for her?"

"You want to look for a rabbit in our basement?"

The two men stared at each other for some time. Ronald

Wilson was wearing a baseball cap, and he took it off and rubbed the top of his head, which was balding. He put the baseball cap back on.

"Your rabbit is not in our house, Mr. Hoffman," Wilson said.

"Okay," Hoffman said. "Okay. Sure."

Hoffman walked back home. He sat at the kitchen table and waited until Ace and Esther were both in the room to make his announcement.

"They took her," he said. "The Wilsons took Bonnie."

Hoffman started to build the tower in July. There was a row of oak trees between Ace Douglas's house and the Wilsons' house, and the leaves from these trees blocked Hoffman's view into their home. For several months, he'd been spending his nights watching the Wilson house from the attic window with binoculars, looking for Bonnie inside, but he could not see into the lower floor rooms for the trees, and was frustrated. Ace reassured him that the leaves would be gone by autumn, but Hoffman was afraid that Bonnie would be dead by autumn. This was difficult for him to take. He was no longer allowed to go over to the Wilsons' property and look into the basement windows, since Ruth-Ann Wilson had called the police. He was no longer allowed to write threatening letters. He was no longer allowed to call the Wilsons on the telephone. He had promised Ace and Esther all of these things.

"He's really harmless," Esther told Ruth-Ann Wilson, although she herself was not sure this was the case.

Ronald Wilson found out somehow that Hoffman had been in prison, and he'd contacted the parole officer, who contacted Hoffman and suggested that he leave the Wilsons alone.

"If you would only let him search your home for the rabbit," Ace Douglas had suggested gently to the Wilsons, "this would be over very quickly. Just give him a half-hour to look around.

It's just that he's concerned that Bonnie is trapped in your basement."

"We did not move here to let murderers into our home," Ronald Wilson said.

"He's not a murderer," Esther protested, somewhat lamely.

"He scares my wife."

"I don't want to scare your wife," Hoffman said.

"He's really harmless," Esther insisted. "Maybe you could buy him a new rabbit."

"I don't want any new rabbit."

"You scare my wife," Ronald repeated. "We don't owe you any rabbit at all."

In late spring, Hoffman cut down the smallest oak tree between the two houses. He did it on a Monday afternoon, when the Wilsons were at work and Esther was performing magic for a Girl Scouts' party and Ace was shopping. Hoffman had purchased a chain saw weeks earlier and had been hiding it. The tree wasn't very big, but it fell at a sharp diagonal across the Wilsons' back yard, narrowly missing their arbor and destroying a substantial corner of the garden.

The police came. After a great deal of negotiating, Ace Douglas was able to prove that the oak tree, while between the two houses, was actually on his property, and it was his right to have it cut down. He offered to pay generously for the damages. Ronald Wilson came over to the house again that night, but he would not speak until Ace sent Hoffman from the room.

"Do you understand our situation?" he asked.

"I do," Ace said. "I honestly do."

The two men sat at the kitchen table across from each other for some time. Ace offered to get Ronald some coffee, which he refused.

"How can you live with him?" Ronald asked.

Ace did not answer this but got himself some coffee. He

opened the refrigerator and pulled out a carton of milk, which he smelled and then poured down the sink. After this, he smelled his cup of coffee, which he poured down the sink, as well.

"Is he your boyfriend?" Ronald asked.

"Is Richard my boyfriend? No. He's my very good friend. And he's my brother-in-law."

"Really," Ronald said. He was working his wedding band around his finger, as though he were screwing it on tight.

"You thought it was a dream come true to buy that nice old house, didn't you?" Ace Douglas asked. He managed to say this in a friendly, sympathetic way.

"Yes, we did."

"But it's a nightmare, isn't it? Living next to us?"

"Yes, it is."

Ace Douglas laughed, and Ronald Wilson laughed, too.

"It's a complete fucking nightmare, actually."

"I'm very sorry that your wife is afraid of us, Ronald."

"Well."

"I truly am."

"Thank you. It's difficult. She's a bit paranoid sometimes."

"Well," Ace said, again in a friendly and sympathetic way. "Imagine that. Paranoid! In this neighborhood?"

The two men laughed again. Meanwhile, in the other room, Esther was talking to her father.

"Why'd you do it, Dad?" she asked. "Such a pretty tree."

He had been weeping.

"Because I am so sad," he said, finally. "I wanted them to feel it."

"To feel how sad you were?" she said.

"To feel how sad I am," he told her. "How sad I am."

Anyway, in July he started to build the tower.

Ace had an old pickup truck, and Hoffman drove it to the

municipal dump every afternoon so that he could look for wood and scrap materials. He built the base of the tower out of pine reinforced with parts of an old steel bed frame. By the end of July, the tower was over ten feet high. He wasn't planning on building a staircase inside, so it was a solid cube.

The Wilsons called the zoning board, which fined Ace Douglas for erecting an unauthorized structure on his property, and insisted that the work stop immediately.

"It's only a tree house," Esther lied to the zoning officer.

"It's a watchtower," Hoffman corrected. "So that I can see into the neighbors' house."

The zoning officer gave Hoffman a long, empty look.

"Yes," Hoffman said. "This truly is a watchtower."

"Take it down," said the zoning officer to Esther. "Take it down immediately."

Ace Douglas owned a significant library of antique magic books, including several volumes that Hoffman himself had brought over from Hungary during the Second World War, and which had been old and valuable even then. Hoffman had purchased these rare books from Gypsies and dealers across Europe with the last of his family's money. Some volumes were written in German, some in Russian, some in English.

The collection revealed the secrets of parlor magic, or drawing room magic, a popular pursuit of educated gentlemen at the turn of the century. The books spoke not of tricks, but of "diversions," which were sometimes magical maneuvers but were just as often simple scientific experiments. Often, these diversions involved hypnosis, or the appearance of hypnosis, or would not be successful without a trained conspirator among the otherwise susceptible guests. A gentleman might literally use smoke and a mirror to evoke a ghost within the parlor. A gentleman might read a palm or levitate a tea tray. A gentleman might simply demonstrate that an egg could stand on its end, or that magnets could react against one another, or that an electric current could turn a small motorized contrivance.

The books were exquisitely illustrated. Hoffman had given them to Ace Douglas back in the 1950s, because he had hoped for some time to re-create this lost European conjury in Pittsburgh. He had hoped to decorate a small area within the Pharaoh's Palace in the manner of a formal upper-middle-class Hungarian drawing room, and to dress Ace in spats and kid gloves. Ace did study the books. But he found that there was no way to accurately replicate most of the diversions. The old tricks all called for common household items which were simply not common anymore: a box of paraffin, a pinch of snuff, a dab of beeswax, a spittoon, a watch fob, a ball of cork, a sliver of saddle soap. Even if such ingredients could be gathered, they would have no meaning to modern spectators. It would be museum magic. It would move nobody.

To Hoffman, this was a considerable disappointment. As a very young man he had watched the Russian charlatan and swindler necromancer Katanovsky perform such diversions in his mother's drawing room. His mother, recently widowed, wore dark gowns decorated with china-blue silk ribbons precisely the same shade as the famous blue vials of Hoffman's Rose Water. Her face was that of a determined regent. His sisters, in childish pinafores, regarded Katanovsky in a pretty stupor of wonder. Gathered in the drawing room as a family, they had all heard it. Hoffman himself — his eyes stinging from phosphorous smoke — had heard it: the unmistakable voice of his recently dead father speaking through Katanovsky's own dark mouth. A father's message (in perfectly accentless Hungarian!) of reassurement. A thrilling, intimate call to faith.

And so it was unfortunate for Hoffman that Ace Douglas could not replicate this diversion. He would've liked to see it tried again. It must have been a very simple swindle, although an antique one. Hoffman would have liked to hear the hoax voice of his dead father repeated and explained to him fully and — if necessary — repeated again.

On the first day of September, Hoffman woke at dawn and began preparing his truck. Months later, during the court proceedings, the Wilsons' attorney would attempt to show that Hoffman had stockpiled weapons in the bed of the truck, an allegation that Esther and Ace would contest heatedly. Certainly there were tools in the truck — a few shovels, a sledgehammer, and an ax — but if these were threatening, they were not so intentionally.

Hoffman had recently purchased several dozen rolls of black electrical duct tape, and at dawn he began winding the tape around the body of the truck. He wound the tape, and then more tape over the existing tape, and he did this again and again, as armor.

Esther had an early-morning flute class to teach, and she got up to eat her cereal. From the kitchen window, she saw her father taping his pickup. The headlights and taillights were already covered and the doors were sealed shut. She went outside.

"Dad?" she said.

And Hoffman said, almost apologetically, "I'm going over there."

"Not to the Wilsons'?"

"I'm going in after Bonnie," he said.

Esther walked back to the house, feeling somewhat shaky. She woke Ace Douglas, who looked from his bedroom window down at Hoffman in the driveway and called the police.

"Oh, not the police," Esther said. "Not the police . . ."

Ace held her in a hug for some time.

"Are you crying?" he asked.

"No," she lied.

"You're not crying?"

"No. I'm just sad."

When the duct tape ran out, Hoffman circled the truck and noticed that he had no way to enter it now. He took the sledge-hammer from the flatbed and lightly tapped the passenger-side window with it, until the glass was evenly spider-webbed. He gently pushed the window in. The glass crystals landed silently on the seat. He climbed inside but noticed that he had no keys, so he climbed out of the broken window again and walked into the house, where he found his keys on the kitchen table. Esther wanted to go downstairs to try to talk to him, but Ace Douglas would not let her go. He went down himself and said, "I'm sorry, Richard. But I've called the police."

"The police?" Hoffman repeated, wounded. "Not the police, Ace."

"I'm sorry."

Hoffman was silent for a long time. Staring at Ace. "But I'm going in there after Bonnie," he said, finally.

"I wish you wouldn't do that."

"But they have her," Hoffman said, and he was weeping.

"I don't believe that they do have her, Richard."

"But they *stole* her!"

Hoffman snatched up his keys and climbed back into his taped-up truck, still weeping. He drove over to the Wilsons' home, and he circled it several times. He drove through the corn in the garden. Ruth-Ann Wilson came running out, and she pulled up some bricks that were lining her footpath, and she chased after Hoffman, throwing the bricks at his truck and screaming.

Hoffman pulled the truck up to the slanting metal basement doors of the Wilsons' house. He tried to drive right up on them, but his truck didn't have the power, and the wheels sank into the wet lawn. He honked in long, forlorn foghorn blasts.

When the police arrived, Hoffman would not come out. He

would, however, put his hands on the steering wheel to show that he was not armed.

"He doesn't have a gun," Esther shouted from within Ace Douglas's house.

Two officers circled the truck and examined it. The younger officer tapped on Hoffman's window and asked him to roll it down, but he refused.

"Tell them to bring her outside!" he shouted. "Bring the rabbit and I will come out of the truck! Terrible people!"

The older officer cut through the duct tape on the passenger-side door with a utility knife. He was able, finally, to open the door, and when he did that, he reached in and dragged Hoffman out, cutting both of their arms on the sparkling glass of the broken window. Outside the truck, Hoffman lay on the grass in a limp sprawl, facedown. He was handcuffed and taken away in a squad car.

Ace and Esther followed the police to the station, where the officers took Hoffman's belt and his fingerprints. Hoffman was wearing only an undershirt, and his cell was small, empty, and chilly.

Esther asked the older police officer, "May I go home and bring my father back a jacket? Or a blanket?"

"You may," said the older police officer, and he patted her arm with a sort of sympathetic authority. "You may, indeed."

Back home, Esther washed her face and took some aspirins. She called the mother of her flute student and canceled that morning's class. The mother wanted to reschedule, but Esther could only promise to call later. She noticed the milk on the kitchen counter and returned it to the refrigerator. She brushed her teeth. She changed into warmer autumn boots, and she went to the living room closet and found a light wool blanket for her father. She heard a noise.

Esther followed the noise, which was that of a running automobile engine. She went to the window of the living room and parted the curtain. In the Wilsons' driveway was a van with markings on the side indicating that it belonged to the ASPCA. There were grills on the windows of this vehicle. Esther said aloud, "Oh, my."

A man in white coveralls came out of the Wilsons' front door, carrying a large wire cage. Inside the cage was Bonnie.

Esther had never been inside the local ASPCA building, and she did not go inside it that day. She parked near the van, which she had followed, and watched as the man in the coveralls opened the back doors and pulled out a cage. This cage held three gray kittens, which he carried into the building, leaving the van doors open.

When the man was safely inside, Esther got out of her car and walked quickly to the back of the van. She found the cage with Bonnie, opened it easily, and pulled out the rabbit. Bonnie was much thinner than last time Esther had seen her, and the rabbit eyed her with an absolutely expressionless gaze of non-recognition. Esther carried Bonnie to her car and drove back to the police station.

Once in *that* parking lot, she tucked the rabbit under her left arm. She got out of the car and wrapped the light wool blanket she'd brought for her father completely around herself. Esther walked briskly into the police station. She passed the older police officer, who was talking to Ace Douglas and Ronald Wilson. She raised her right hand as she walked near the men and said solemnly, "How, palefaces."

Ace smiled at her, and the older police officer waved her by.

Hoffman's jail cell was at the end of a hallway, and it was poorly lit. Hoffman had not been sleeping well for several weeks, and he was cold and cut. The frame of his glasses was cracked, and he had been weeping since that morning. He saw Esther approaching, wrapped in the light gray wool blanket, and he saw in her the figure of his mother, who had worn cloaks against the Budapest winters and had also walked with a particular dignity.

Esther approached the cell, and she reached her hand between the bars toward her father, who rose with a limp to meet that hand. In a half-mad moment, he half-imagined her to be a warm apparition of his mother, and, as he reached for her, she smiled.

Her smile directed his gaze from her hand to her face, and in that instant, Esther pulled her arm back out of the cell, reached into the folds of the blanket around her, and gracefully produced the rabbit. She slid Bonnie — slimmer now, of course — through the iron bars and held the rabbit aloft in the cell, exactly where her empty hand had been only a moment before. Such that Hoffman, when he glanced down from Esther's smile, saw a rabbit where before there had been no rabbit at all. Like a true enchantment, something appeared from the common air.

"Behold," suggested Esther.

Richard Hoffman beheld the silken rabbit and recognized her as his Bonnie. He collected her into his square hands. And then, after that, he did behold his own daughter Esther.

A most gifted young woman.

The Finest Wife

✦ ✦ ✦

W HEN ROSE was sixteen years old and five months pregnant, she won a beauty pageant in South Texas, based
on her fine walk up a runway in a sweet navy-blue
bathing suit. This was shortly before the war. She had been a
skinny, knee-scratching kid only the summer earlier, but her
pregnancy had just delivered her this sudden prize of a body. It
was as though life was gestating in her thighs and ass and
breasts, not in her belly. It might have seemed that she was
carrying all the soft weights of motherhood spread evenly and
perfect across her whole frame. Those parts of herself that she
could not quite pack into the blue bathing suit spilled over it
exactly enough to emotionally disturb several of the judges and
spectators. She was an uncontested champion beauty.

Rose's father, too, saw the pin-up shape that his daughter had
taken, and, five months too late, he started worrying about the
maintenance of her graces. Soon after the pageant, her condi-
tion became obvious. Her father sent her to a facility in Oklahoma, where she stayed until she experienced four days of labor
and the delivery of a stillborn son. Rose could not actually have
any more children after that, but the lovely figure was hers to

keep, and she ended up eventually married, once again on the basis of a fine walk in a sweet bathing suit.

But she didn't meet her husband until the war was over. In the meantime, she stayed in Oklahoma. She had developed a bit of a taste for certain types of tall, smiling local men in dark hats. Also, she had developed a taste for certain types of church-going men and also for left-handed men, and for servicemen, fishermen, postmen, assemblymen, firemen, highwaymen, elevator repairmen, and the Mexican busboys at the restaurant where she worked (who reverently called her La Rubia — the Blond — as if she were a notorious bandit or a cardsharp).

She married her husband because she loved him best. He was kind to waitresses and dogs, and was not in any way curious about her famous tastes. He was a big man himself, with a rump like the rump of a huge animal — muscled and hairy. He dialed telephones with pencil stubs because his fingers didn't fit the rotary holes. He smoked cigarettes that looked like shreds of toothpicks against the size of his mouth. He couldn't fall asleep without feeling Rose's bottom pressed up warm against his belly. He held her as if she were a puppy. In the years after they got a television, they would watch evening game shows together on the couch, and he would genuinely applaud the contestants who had won cars and boats. He was happy for them. He would clap for them with his big arms stretched out stiffly, the way a trained seal claps.

They moved to Minnesota, eventually. Rose's husband bought a musky flock of sheep and a small, tight house. She was married to him for forty-three years, and then he died of a heart attack. He was quite a bit older than she was, and he had lived a long time. Rose thought that he had passed the kind of life after which you should say, "Yes! That was a good one!" Her mourning was appreciative and fond.

When he was gone, the sheep became too much work, and she sold them off, a few at a time. And when the sheep were all gone — spread across several states as pets, yarn, dog food, and mint-jellied chops — Rose became the driver of the local kindergarten school bus. She was damn near seventy years old.

Rose was no longer easy with names, but her eyes were good, and she was a careful driver, as she always had been. They gave her an excellent route of kindergartners. First, she would pick up the bus itself, at the station behind the gravel pits, over the double paths of train tracks. Then she would pick up the neighbor boy, who lived by the gas station near Rose's own house. Then she'd pick up the crying boy. Then she'd pick up the girl whose mother always dressed her in corduroy vests, then the boy who looked like Orson Welles, then the disgusted girl, then the humming boy, then the girl with all the Band-Aids. At the bridge by the Band-Aid girl's house, she would cross the river to the hill road. There, she'd pick up the black girl, the grateful-looking boy, the shoving boy, the other black girl, and the out-of-breath girl. Last stop was the absent boy.

Thirteen passengers. Twelve, if you didn't count the absent boy, as Rose tended not to.

But on the particular morning that makes this story, the neighbor boy, the crying boy, and the corduroy vest girl were all absent. Rose thought, *Flu?* She kept on driving and found the Orson Welles boy and the disgusted girl and the humming boy absent also, and she wondered, *Chicken pox?* After the bridge passed with no girl on it, and the whole hill road passed with no children near it, she thought, with some humiliation, *Could today be Sunday?* She recalled, then, having seen no other bus drivers at the gravel pit station, nor any other school bus crossing the double paths of railroad tracks. She had not, in fact, noticed any other cars on the roads at all. Not that these were fast highways, but they were certainly driven roads. They were always used roads. And Rose thought lightly, *Armageddon?*

But she rode her route out to the end. It was a fine choice that she did, too, because there was someone at the bottom of the absent boy's driveway, after all. Two people, in fact, waiting for her. She stopped the bus, demonstrated the proper and legal flashing lights, cranked the door open, and let them in. They were two very old men, one short, one tall. It took them some trouble to get up the stairs.

"A ride for you gentlemen today?" she asked.

They sat in the seat just behind her own.

"It smells clean and decent in here, thank God," one of them said.

"I use a tub and tile cleaner," Rose answered. "Weekly."

The taller man said, "My sweet Rosie. You look terrific."

As a matter of fact, she did. She wore a hat and white gloves to work every day, as if she were driving those school children to church or to some important picnic.

"You could be a first lady," the tall one went on. "You could have married a president."

She looked at him in the wide, easy reflection of her rearview mirror, and then gave a pretty little expression of surprise and recognition. She looked at the shorter man and made the expression again. And this is who they were: Tate Palinkus and Dane Ladd. Tate was the man who had knocked her up back in South Texas before the war. Dane had been an orderly whom she had often kissed and fondled during her recovery from childbirth, at the Oklahoma Institution for Unwed Mothers. Which was also before the war.

"Won't I be damned?" she said. "I sure never thought I'd see either of you two again. And right here in Minnesota. How nice."

Dane said, "Ain't this Tate Palinkus nothing but a Christless old bastard? He's just been telling me about getting you pregnant."

Tate said, "Rose. I did not know that you were pregnant at

the time. I did not even hear about that until many years later, when I came around asking for you. That is the truth, Rose."

"Tate Palinkus," she said. "You big bugger."

Dane said, "Foolin' around on a fifteen-year-old girl. I guess that's about the worst thing I ever heard of."

"Dane Ladd." Rose smiled. "You big stinker."

"She was a hell of a pretty girl," Tate said, and Dane said, "You barely have to remind me of that."

Rose shifted her bus and turned it around.

She said, "You two have surprised my face just about off my body."

"Don't lose that sweet face," Dane said. "Don't lose that sweet body."

They drove on. And, as it turned out, there was someone waiting at the end of the out-of-breath girl's driveway, leaning on the mailbox. Another very old man. Rose stopped and let him on.

"Precious," he called her, and he touched the brim of his hat. He was Jack Lance-Hainey, a deacon of the Presbyterian church. He had once run an Oklahoma senatorial campaign. He used to take Rose out for picnics during the 1940s, with baskets full of his wife's real china and real silver. He had taught Rose how to climb on top of a man during sex, and how to pick up phones in hotel rooms and say, "This is Mrs. Lance-Hainey. Might you send me up a bottle of tonic for my terrible, terrible headache?"

Jack sat on the seat across the aisle from the other men, and set his hat beside him.

"Mr. Ladd." He nodded. "It's a beautiful morning."

"It is," Dane agreed. "What a fine country we live in."

"It is a fine country," Jack Lance-Hainey said, and added, "And good morning to you, Tate Palinkus, you fertile and lecherous old son of a snake."

"I did not know she was pregnant at the time, Jack," Tate explained. "Not until years later. I would have happily married her."

And Rose said, under her breath, "Well, well, well . . . That *is* news, Mr. Palinkus."

Now she rode her abandoned bus route backward, and found it fully packed with all her old lovers. She picked up every single one of them. At the house of the black girl, she picked up her Mississippi cousin Carl, who she had once met on an aunt's bed during a Thanksgiving gathering. By the shoving boy's mailbox, she found a small crowd of old men, waiting together. They were all of her postmen, out of uniform. They had all once driven airy trucks and kept stacks of extra canvas bags in the back for her to lie down on. She couldn't remember their names, but the other men on the bus seemed to know them well, and they greeted one another with professional politeness.

At the other black girl's house, she picked up two elderly veterans, who she remembered as enlisted men, their young scalps pink and shaved, their big ears tempting handles for tugging and guiding. The veterans sat behind Lane and Tate and talked about the economy. One of them was missing an arm and one was missing a leg. The armless one punched Tate with his good arm suddenly and said, "You're just a lousy, no-good, knock-'em-up-and-leave-'em old prick, aren't you?"

"He claims he didn't know that she was pregnant," Jack Lance-Hainey said, and the postmen all laughed in disbelief.

"I did not know she was pregnant at the time," Tate said patiently. "Not until years later."

"My God," Rose said, "I barely knew it myself."

"That baby got you that nice figure," Tate offered, and a shared murmur of endorsement at this thought passed throughout the bus.

At the grateful girl's house, she picked up a man so fat he had to reintroduce himself. He was her sister's first husband, he said, and Rose said, "Coach! You troublemaker!" He had been an elevator mechanic, who used to meet Rose in the shop at night to teach her how to trick-shuffle a deck of cards and how to kiss with her eyes open.

"Those steps are lethal," he said, red-faced from the climb, and the one-legged veteran said, "Who you tellin', Coach?"

At the Band-Aid girl's house, she picked up the bartenders from three states who she had fallen for, and at the humming boy's house, she picked up a highway patrolman she'd spent a night with in Oklahoma City, back when they were both young. He was with a shrimp fisherman and a man who used to drive fire engines. They let him on the bus first, because they thought he had rank.

"Ma'am," the highway patrolman called her, and smiled wide. Then he called Tate Palinkus a bad egg, a bad seed, a lowlife, a ruffian, and a dirt bag for getting her pregnant, back when she was just a kid who didn't know a worthless son of a bitch from a fruit bowl.

There was an Arizona circuit court judge waiting for her at the end of the disgusted girl's driveway, and he sat down, with Jack Lance-Hainey, in the front of the bus. He told Rose she still looked good enough to crawl up under his robe any day of the week.

She said, "Your Honor, we are old people now."

He said, "You're a daisy, Rose."

She found Hank Spellman kicking rocks around the road in front of the Orson Welles boy's house. He got on the bus, and the other men cheered, "Hank!" as if they were truly pleased to see him. Hank once sold and installed furnaces, and he had always been a popular man. He used to dance with Rose in her cellar, keeping time by tapping his hand on her hip. He used to slide his hands over her as they danced. He used to take big handfuls of her bottom and whisper to her, "If I'm ever missing and you need to find me, you can start looking for me right here on this ass."

Where the girl who always wore a corduroy vest usually waited for the bus, there was a tall old man in a dark hat. He had once been Rose's dentist. He'd had an indoor swimming pool and a maid, who would bring them towels and cocktails all night without comment. He had to use a cane to get on the bus, and his glasses were as thick as slices of bread. He told Rose that she was beautiful and that her figure was still a wonder.

Rose said, "Thank you very much. I've been lucky with my looks. The women in my family tend to age in one of two ways. Most of them either look like they smoked too many cigarettes or like they ate too many doughnuts."

"You look like you kissed too many boys," the elevator mechanic said.

"You could have been a first lady," Lane said again, and Tate said thoughtfully, "You were my lady first."

There were four former Mexican busboys standing by the picket fence of the crying boy's house. They were old now, and identical, each one of them in a pressed white suit with handsome white hair and a white mustache.

"La Rubia," they called her in turn. Their English was no better than it had ever been, but the armless veteran had fought Fascists in Spain, and he translated quite well.

This was the most crowded that her bus had ever been. It was not a very large bus. It was just for kindergartners, and, to be honest, it was just for the morning class of kindergartners. Naturally, the bus company had given Rose an excellent route, but it was not such a strenuous one. She was generally finished by noon. She was damn near seventy, of course, and although she was certainly not a weak woman, not a senile woman, she did get tired. So they had given her only those thirteen children so close to her own house. She was doing a wonderful job, a truly excellent job. Everyone agreed. She was a careful and polite driver. One of the better ones.

She rode her whole route backward that day, with all of the old men lovers on her kindergarten bus with her. She drove all the way without seeing one of her children and without passing another car. She had decided, with some shame, that it might very well be Sunday. She had never made such a mistake before, and would not consider mentioning it to her old lovers, or they might think she was getting dim. So she rode the whole route right back to the very first stop, which was the house of the neighbor boy, who lived by the gas station near her own home. There was an old man waiting there, too, and he was a rather large man. He was actually her husband. The old men lovers on the bus, who seemed to know each other so beautifully, did not know Rose's husband at all. They were quiet and respectful as he got on the bus, and Rose cranked the door shut behind him and said, "Gentlemen? I'd like to you meet my husband."

And the look on her husband's face was the look of a man at a welcome surprise party. He leaned down to kiss her on the forehead, and he was the first of the men who had touched her that day. He said, "My sweet little puppy of a Rose." She kissed his cheek, which was musky, sheepy, and familiar.

She drove on. He stepped down the aisle of the bus, which rocked like a boat, and he was the guest of honor. The old men lovers introduced themselves, and after each introduction, Rose's husband said, "Ah, yes, of course, how nice to meet you," keeping his left hand on his heart in wonder and pleasure. She watched, in the wide, easy reflection of her rearview mirror, as they patted his back and grinned. The veterans saluted him, and the highway patrolman saluted him, and Jack Lance-Hainey kissed his hand. Tate Palinkus apologized for getting Rose pregnant when she was just a South Texas kid, and the white-haired Mexican busboys struggled with their English greetings.

The circuit court judge said that he did not mind speaking for everyone by saying how simply delighted he was to congratulate Rose and her husband on their long and honest marriage.

Rose kept on driving. Soon, she was at the double paths of railroad tracks that came right before the gravel pit bus station. Her little bus fit exactly between those two sets of tracks, and she stopped in that narrow space because she noticed that trains were coming from both directions. Her husband and her old men lovers pulled down the windows of the bus and leaned out like kindergartners, watching. The trains were painted bright like wooden children's toys, and stenciled on the sides of each boxcar in block letters were the freight contents: APPLES, BLANKETS, CANDY, DIAMONDS, EXPLOSIVES, FABRIC, GRAVY, HAIRCUTS — a continuing, alphabetical account of all a life's ingredients.

They watched this for a long time. But those boxcars were moving slowly, and repeating themselves in new, foreign alphabets. So the old men lovers became bored, finally, and pulled up the windows of Rose's bus for some quietness. They rested and waited, stuck as they were between those two lazy trains. And Rose, who had been up early that morning, took the key out of the ignition, took off her hat and her gloves, and went to sleep. The old men lovers talked about her husband among themselves, fascinated. They whispered low to each other, but she could hear some pieces of words. "Hush," she kept hearing them say, and "shh" and "she" and "and." And, murmured together, those pieces of words made a sound just like the whole word "husband." That's the word she was hearing, in any case, as she dozed on the bus, with all of her old men together and behind her and so pleased just to see her again.